Seeing France with

Seeing France with Uncle John

by Anne Warner

YVONNE TO HER MOTHER

Second day out at sea.

   Dear Mama: We did get off at last, about four in the afternoon, but you never imagined anything like the day we had with Uncle John. It was awful, and, as luck would have it, he just happened to go aft or sou'west, or whatever it is on shipboard, in time to see them drop his trunk into the hold, and they let it fall from such a height that he swore for an hour. I don't see why Uncle is so unreasonable; a Russian gentleman had the locks broken to both his trunks and just smiled, and a very lovely Italian lady had her trunk caved in by the hoisting-rope and only shrugged her shoulders; but Uncle turned the whole deck fairly black and blue on account of a little fall into the hold. If Lee had only been along to soothe him down! But Lee is in London by this time. I do think he might have waited and gone with us, but Uncle says he's glad he didn't, because he says he has more than half an idea that Lee's in love with me, and that no girl alive could be happy with him. I wish Uncle liked Lee better. I wish Lee wouldn't slap him on the back and call him "old boy" the way he does.

   Mrs. Clary doesn't like it because she has to sit next to the doctor and talk English to him, and he can't talk English. She says whenever she goes on board a liner the doctor always spots her as intelligent-looking, and has her put next to him for English purposes. She says she's made seven trips as nursery-governess to a doctor with linguistic aspirations. The consequence is, she has most of her meals on deck with a man named Mr. Chopstone. Uncle doesn't like Mr. Chopstone, because he says he has a sneaking suspicion that Mr. Chopstone admires Edna. He says Edna could never be happy with a man like Mr. Chopstone.

   More later.

Fourth day out.

I've been writing Lee; I can mail it at Plymouth. It does seem to me as if Lee might have waited and gone with us.

We are nicely adjusted now, and Uncle has had his trunk brought to his room, and has examined the corners and found them intact; so now the trunk is off his mind. But he has almost had fits over a man named Monsieur Sibilet, so the situation has been about as brimstony as ever. M. Sibilet is a Frenchman going back to France, but his chair is next to Mrs. Clary's, and Uncle says steamer-chairs are never accidents, but are always premeditated and with intent to kill. He asked Mrs. Clary if she couldn't see that no woman could ever be happy with a dancing fan-tan like Sibilet. We didn't know what a "fan-tan" was, but we all agreed with Uncle's premises as to poor monsieur; and then it developed that there is a Mme. Sibilet deathly sick down below, and Uncle said that he had known it all the time and was only joking.

Edna and Harry are very happy, but they have to be awfully careful, because Uncle says he has a half-fledged notion that Harry is paying attention to Edna, and that he won't allow anything of the kind—not for one York second. We don't know what a "York second" is, and we haven't asked. Uncle plays poker nights, and we make the most of it. There is a nice Yale man on board, and I walk around with him. His name is Edgar. Uncle says he looks as if he had his bait out for a fortune, but Mrs. Clary says to never mind it—to go right on walking. She lies still while we walk, ande talks to M. Sibilet in French.

"She lies still and talks to M. Sibilet"

"While we walk"

Uncle says he is the head of this expedition, and there's to be no foolishness. He says it's all rot about a man not being able to see through women, and that Edna and I needn't expect to keep any secrets from him. I do wish Lee was here to soothe him down. He was so furious to-day because he shut up his wash-stand and let the tooth-powder slide to perdition. M. Sibilet offered him an extra box of his own, but Uncle wasn't a bit grateful. He says he is sure M. Sibilet is in love with Mrs. Clary now, or why under the sun should he offer him his tooth-powder? He says he thinks it's disgraceful, considering poor Mme. Sibilet, and he took mine instead.

More later.

Sixth day out.

I do wish we were in Havre, or anywhere where Uncle had more room. The third officer invited him up on the bridge yesterday, and Uncle says you needn't tell him that any third officer in this world ever would invite him up to the bridge unless he had his eye on Edna or me. Uncle says for Edna and me to remember that old uncles have eyes as well as young third officers, and to bear in mind that it would be a dog's life to be married to a third officer. I'm beginning to be very glad, indeed, that Lee took another steamer; I reckon Lee saw how it would be. Uncle says he'd like to know what we took a slow steamer for, anyhow. He says it would have been more comfortable to have all been in death agonies and to have been in Havre by this time. He was terribly upset to-day by Mme. Sibilet's coming on deck and proving to be an old lady with white hair and the mother of monsieur instead of the wife. He says you needn't talk to him about French honor after this. We don't know what the connection is between poor old Mme. Sibilet and French honor, but we think it best not to ask. The truth is, Uncle lost all patience with M. Sibilet the day it rained and pitched—I think it was the third day out. He never did like him very much, anyhow. Mrs. Clary wanted to sit in the wind that day, and she and monsieur sat in the wind until the rain grew so bad that they were absolutely driven to come around and sit by Uncle, under the lee of the port, or whatever it is on board ship. Monsieur lugged Mrs. Clary's chair because he couldn't find a steward, and he brought it around by the smoking-room and the whole length of the deck, with the steamer pitching so that half the time he was on top of the chair, and the other half of the time the chair was on top of him. There was no one on deck but us, on account of the storm, and I thought we should die laughing, because there were forty empty chairs under shelter already. Uncle waited until, with a final slip and a slide, the poor man landed the chair, and then he screamed: "I say, Sibbilly, just take the cards out and change *them* another time. That's the way we Americans do."

You should have seen poor monsieur's face! Uncle said the whole affair gave him a queer feeling as to what might be in store for us in France. He said if M. Sibilet was a sample Frenchman, he thought he wouldn't get off at Havre, after all.

Mrs. Clary is in lots of trouble over the doctor. He comes up on deck and bothers her half to death, talking English. She can't understand his English, and M. Sibilet gets tired translating. M. Sibilet speaks seven languages. Uncle says that's nothing to his credit, however.

More later.

Ninth day out.

Uncle is in high spirits to-day, for he won the pool. He has been so disgusted because Mr. Edgar has won it three times. Uncle says that's no sign he'd be a good husband, though. I do think Uncle's logic is so very peculiar. He came into my state-room to-day and asked me if I didn't think the doctor was absolutely impertinent in the way he was pursuing Mrs. Clary. You'd have thought the doctor tore after her around the deck, to hear him. He said he expected to have trouble with Edna and me, but he never looked for Mrs. Clary to be a care. He said he didn't suppose she was over forty, but she ought to consider appearances more. He was quite put out, and I am gladder than ever that Lee isn't with us.

We laughed ourselves half sick to-day over Mr. Chopstone. Uncle's port-hole doesn't work very easily, and Mr. Chopstone heard him talking about it to himself as he passed in the corridor, and he went in to help him. Uncle asked Mr. Chopstone if he had a crow-bar or a monkey-wrench with him, and Mr. Chopstone didn't have a crow-bar or a monkey-wrench with him, but said why not ring for the steward. Uncle wouldn't hear to the steward, and so they climbed on the divan together and tried to pry it with Uncle's hair-brush.

The hair-brush broke, and Uncle went spinning, but Mr. Chopstone caught his cuff in the crack, and it tore, and half of his shirt-sleeve with a diamond cuff-link went to sea. At first we all felt awful about it, but he was so composed that Edna said he must be a millionaire, and Uncle said it must be a paste diamond. That is all only preliminary to the funny part. This afternoon we were lying in our chairs and Uncle was standing by the rail looking at a ship. All of a sudden he exclaimed, "Great Scott! Chopstone, if there isn't your cuff!" Mr. Chopstone made just one bound from his chair to the rail, and looked over so hard that his cap fell into the sea. Of course the mere idea of the cuff having sailed as fast as we did all day used us up completely, and Uncle in particular had to hang to the rail for support while he sort of wove back and forth in an ecstasy of speechless joy. Even M. Sibilet was overcome by mirth, although it turned out afterward that he thought the fun was on account of the lost cap. And then, when we got ourselves selves under control once more, Mr. Chopstone explained that what he had thought was that the cuff had caught somewhere on the outside of the steamer and that Uncle saw it hanging there. Edna says that it all shows that poor Mr. Chopstone is *not* a millionaire, and Mrs. Clary says it proves, too, that it *was* a real diamond.

It is beginning to seem like a pretty long trip, and Mrs. Clary has started packing her trunk. The little flag that marks our progress across the chart is making Europe in great jumps, and we are all glad. Uncle gets more restless every day, and he says if the doctor don't quit coming up on deck to talk to Mrs. Clary, something will soon drop. The doctor is really very amusing; he says the first officer has a pet "marmadillo," but we cannot see it because it is too anxious. He means "frightened," it seems. Mr. Edgar is very nice; both he and Mr. Chopstone are going to Paris. Lee will be in Paris by Wednesday, I hope, and I most sincerely trust he will keep on the right side of Uncle.

They say we will land early day after to-morrow. I can mail my letters in Plymouth to-morrow evening. Uncle says he's going express hereafter; he says no more dilly-dally voyages for him.

Tenth day out.

What do you think! Uncle took me into the parlor after dinner to-night and told me that he wasn't going to Paris with the rest. He says he didn't come abroad to scurry around like a wild rabbit, and that he's going to stop in Havre for a day or two. He says Edna and I had better stay with him, as he can't think of our traveling with Mr. Edgar and Mr. Chopstone alone. I said, "But there's Mrs. Clary." And he said, "Yes; but you forget Sibbilly." I do think Uncle's logic is so remarkable.

Eleventh day out.

Everybody is getting their trunks in from the baggage-room and running to the rail to look at ships. Uncle won the pool again to-day; he says this is one of the pleasantest trips he ever made, and he shook hands with M. Sibilet when he met him on deck this morning.

Mrs. Clary is awfully upset over our staying in Havre, and she says if Lee is in Paris he won't like it, either. We expect a mail in Plymouth.

Later.

The mail came, and I had a letter from Lee. He is going to Russia for a week, and he folded in an extra piece, saying to give Uncle the letter. It was a funny kind of letter, but of course it had to be a funny kind of letter if I was to give it to Uncle. I gave it to Uncle, and he said, "Hum!" and that was all. He says if Mr. Edgar or Mr. Chopstone stay in Havre he'll know the reason why. I do think Uncle might be more reasonable. Edna has been crying. She doesn't want to stay in Havre; she wants to go to Paris when Harry goes.

Yours with love, as ever,

Yvonne.

UNCLE JOHN IN ROUEN

9 a.m.

"Well, girls, are you ready to get up and out and set about improving your minds? I've been reading the guide-book and spilling my coffee with trying to do two things at once, ever since eight o'clock. But what your Uncle John doesn't know about Rouen now isn't worth stopping to look up in the index. Why, I've even got the real French twang to the pronunciation. It's Rooank; only you stop short of the 'n' and the 'k,' so to speak. The waiter who brought my breakfast showed me how to do it—said he never saw a foreigner catch on to the trick so quick before. I gave him one of those slim little quarters they have here, and he was so pleased that he taught me how to say 'Joan of Arc' for nothing. It's Shondark—*Shondark*. I learned it in no time. Well, come on, if you're ready. I've been waiting almost an hour.

Rouen—Maison du XV siècle

"I declare, but this fresh, free atmosphere is refreshing! As soon as you get outside of your bedroom door you begin to get the full benefit of the Continental climate. I presume, if you're poor, you get it as soon as you get outside of your bed clothes. Rather a medieval staircase, eh? And four orange-trees at the bottom to try and fool us into feeling balmy. However, I don't mind little discomforts: all I mind is being shut up on a ship with a darned fool like that man Sibbilly. I shouldn't wonder if his mother was his wife, after all. I could believe anything of him. I didn't like him.

"We'll go to take in the cathedral first; it isn't far, and I've got it all by heart. Thirteenth century and unsymmetrical—you must remember that. There, that's it ahead there—with the scaffolding. They're bolstering it up somewhat, so as to keep on hooking tourists, I presume. The biggest tower is the Butter Tower, built out of paid-for permissions to eat butter in Lent. Rather a rough joke, its being so much the biggest, isn't it? The whole cathedral's lopsided from eating butter, so to speak. I believe it's the thing to stop in front and act as if you were overcome; so we'll just call a halt here and take in the general effect of the scaffolding.

"Now we'll walk around the whole thing. I haven't come abroad to take life with a hop, skip, and jump; I've come to be thorough, and I want you girls to form the habit of being thorough, too. What I didn't like about that fellow Edgar was his not being thorough. When he went down to look at the ship's machinery he only stayed an hour. Now, I didn't go at all; but if I had gone, I should have stayed more than an hour. Good job of scaffolding, isn't it? You see, they make the scaffolding out of young trees withed together, and use them over and over. Economical. Just about what you'd expect of Sibbilly. Those gargoyles and saints around the top stick their heads out pretty interested-like, don't they? But their view is for the most part blocked. Now this cheerful old jail at the back is the palace of the archbishop. I wish, young ladies, that you would note those little bits of high windows and the good thick bars across them as illustrating the secure faith that the dead and gone archbishops had in their loving people. I'll bet there's been plenty of battering and rioting around under these walls, first and last; plenty of fists and sticks and stones. It's big, isn't it? Big as half a block, and things look so much bigger here than they do at home.

They slide a roof up slanting and cock it full of little crooked windows, and you feel as if you must tip over backward to take in the top. I vow, I don't just see how it's done; but—oh, here's where we go in. This dark, damp little stone-paved alley is the celebrated 'Portail des Libraires,' so called because those arcades used to be full of book-stalls. We go along on the cobble-stones,ont throw ourselves hard against this little swinging door; it creaks, it yields, we enter—hush!

"Great Scott, isn't it big, and *isn't* it damp? Will you look up in that roof? I feel solemn in spite of myself; but, then, feeling solemn is no use: what we want to do is to find some one to open those big iron gates, for the most of what is to see is in back there. Edna, you ask that man how we can get hold of some other man. Well, what did he say? Said to ask the Swiss, did he? What does he mean by that? Is it a joke, or can't they trust a Frenchman with their old relics? I've been told that in Japanese banks they always have to have a Chinaman to handle the money, and maybe it's equally the thing in a French cathedral to have a Swiss look after the relics. But the guide-book never said a word about a Swiss: it said '*fee*,' and I've got my pocket full of them.

"Well, where can we get a Swiss? I should think he'd be more handy than he appears to be. There's another man looking for him, too. He—Great Scott! if it isn't—no, that is impossible. Yes, it is!

"I beg your pardon, sir, but is your name Porter? Yes? Robert Porter—Bobby Porter that went to the Washington School? Bob, do you remember me? Well, of all the larks!

"Girls, this man and I went to school side by side for eight years, and he's the finest—my nieces, Bob. That's Edna and this is Yvonne, and—you don't say he's your son? Didn't know you ever married. Oh, I'll take your word for it, of course; but, I say, Bob, you've got to come and dine with us to-night. You must; I won't have it any other way. You and I'll have to just sit down and overhaul all our old memories together. Do you remember—but how do you come to be in Europe, anyhow; and what liner did you line up on? We had a beastly trip,—only came from Havre last night,—and, by the way, how in thunder can we get hold of the man who opens these iron gates? Everything in the place is back there.

"Is that a Swiss—that splendid circus-chariot driver? Give you my word, I thought he was a cardinal! How much of a tip is that much gold lace going to look forward to getting? I wish he was plainer, somehow. I'll tell you, Bob; you pay, and I'll settle up later. I certainly am glad to see the gates open; I felt more like a serpent shut out of paradise than I ever expected to feel in all my life.

"Well, now we begin. Who's buried here? Henry II of England, eh? I can't read Latin, so Henry's virtues and dates are all one to me. Which Henry was he, anyhow—the one with six wives or the one who never shed a smile? Either way, let's move on.

"What comes next? Richard-Cœur-de-Lion—petrified, eh? Oh, only a statue of him; that's less interesting. I thought at last I was looking at Richard when he was himself again. What is our Swiss friend hissing about? Heart buried underneath? Whose heart?—Richard's? Ask if it's his bona fide heart or only a death-mask of it? Strikes me as a pretty big statue to put up to a heart, don't you think, Bob? But come on; I want to be looking at something else.

"'Richard-Cœur-de-Lion—petrified, eh?'"

"So this is the tomb of the husband of Diana of Poitiers? I didn't know she ever had a husband—thought she only had a king. I've never been brought up to think of Diana of Poitiers mourning a husband. But maybe she did, maybe she did. They say you must check your common sense at the hotel when you set out to inspect Europe, and I believe it—I believe it. It's a nice tomb, and if they kneel and mourn in a gown with a train, she certainly is doing it up brown. However, let's go on.

"Two cardinals of Amboise kind of going in procession on their knees over their own dead bodies—or maybe it's only hearts again. Well, Bob, the Reformation was a great thing, after all, wasn't it? Must have felt fine to straighten up for a while. Stop a bit; the guide-book said there was something to examine about these two—wait till I find the place. Oh, well, never mind; I dare say a guide-book's very handy, but I move we quit this damp old hole, anyway. I wouldn't bother to come again. That's a sad thing about life, Bob; as soon as you get in front of anything and get a square look at it, you're ready to move on—at least I am.

"What's he saying? Well, ask him again. Whose grave? Well, ask him again. Rollo's! What, Rollo that was 'At Work' and 'At Play' and at everything else when we were kids? Another? What other? Well, ask him. Rollo the Norman? I don't see anything very remarkable in a Norman being buried in Normandy, do you, Bob? When did he die? Well, *ask* him. What are we paying him for, anyway? Died about 900, eh! And this church wasn't built till four hundred years later. Where did he spend the time while he was waiting to be buried? Well, ask him. I declare, if I could talk French, I bet I'd know something about things. You are the *dumbest* lot! Here's Rollo lying around loose for as long as we've had America with us, and no one takes any interest in where. Is that the tomb he finally got into? Clever idea to have it so dark no one can see it, after all. I suppose he thinks we'll be impressed, but I ain't. I don't believe Rollo's in there, anyhow.

"Come on; I'm tired of this old church. I move that we go out and look at the place where they burned Joan of Arc, or something else that is bright and cheerful. What's he saying? No, I don't want to see any treasury; I've done enough church-going for one week-day. Give him his money, Bob, and let's get out. You tell us where to go next; you must know everything, if you were here all day yesterday. I want to see that double-faced clock and those carvings of the Field of the Cloth of Gold. They're all over in the same direction.

"Good to be out in the air, eh? I vow, I never was great on churches. What boat did you come over on? Did it roll? Ours rolled and pitched, too. I never saw such a rolling. I tell you, Bob, the man will make a fortune who invents a level liner. I used to try and figure on how to hang the passenger department in an open square, so it could swing free,—do you get the idea?—but I don't know as it could be managed. I was trying to work it out one morning, and I came up against the wash-stand so sudden that I thought I was cut in two; the next second I went backward so quick that the edge of the berth nearly amputated my legs; and then the whole craft arose on such a swell that I swallowed half my toothbrush. You may laugh, Bob, but I'm not telling this to be funny; I'm telling it for a fact. I had to have the steward in to put the washing-apparatus to rights, and I asked him what in thunder was up outside. He was standing at an angle of forty-five degrees, looking up at me where I sat in the lower berth, and he said, 'If the wind shifts, we're very likely to have it rough.' Just then he took on an angle of ninety-five degrees, and my trunk slid out on his feet so quick he had to hop. I said: 'Have it *rough*, eh? Well, I'm glad to know, so that I can take advantage of this calm spell.'

"'So that's the clock!'"

"So that's the clock! Well, it's a big one, surely—almost as wide as the street, although candor compels us to own that the street is about the narrowest ever. All right, I'm done; a clock is a clock, and one look in its face always tells me all I want to know. Come on; we can't stand dilly-dallying if we're to get through Rouen to-day, and I must say I consider a day to a town as quite enough in Europe. I know, when I was young and traveled for wholesale shoes, I used often and often to do three towns a day and never turn a hair. I tell you, Bob, when I was—

"Is that the fountain? Hold on; we want to see that! The guide-book has it in italics. I don't see anything to underline, though; looks foreign to me. Come on; we've got to be getting somewhere, or I shall feel I was a fool to stop off at Rouen. Not that I'm not glad to have met you again, Bob; but that could have happened anywhere else just as well, you know. When did you come over? Last year! Great Scott, what are you staying so long for? I bet I get enough in six weeks; I feel as if I'd got pretty close to enough now. Not that time ever hangs heavy on my hands, you know. No, not by a long shot. I'm the kind of man that can always amuse himself. Give me a fair show,—off a ship, of course,—and I'll defy any one to get on better. Take the day we landed, for instance, there in Havre,—rainy, not a thing to do, and every one else off for Paris. You might have looked for me to be a little disgusted, naturally; but not a bit of it. The day went like the wind. We landed at noon, I slept all the afternoon, and in the evening I took a bath. I tell you, Bob, a fellow with brains can get on anywhere. I never know what it is to feel bored.

"What's our Goddess of Liberty doing up there? What's that Indian beadwork around her feet for? Who? You don't mean to tell me that's Joan of Arc? Well, all I can say is, I never imagined her like that. But what are the beads? French funeral wreaths! Great Scott! do they keep Charlemagne wreathed, too, or is five hundred years the bead-wreath limit? Pretty idea, to put up a fountain where they burnt her—keep her memory damp at all events, eh? What's the moral of her train turning into a dolphin? Just to bring the mind gradually down to the level of the fact that it is a fountain, after all, I suppose.

"She wasn't burnt here, anyhow, the book said. The book said she was burnt farther over. Smart people here—have two places where she was burnt, so people must trot through the whole market if they try to be conscientious. Look at that woman, with her bouquet of live chickens—novel effect in chickens, eh, Bob? Strikes me it was an enterprising idea to burn Joan in the market, anyhow— good business for the market. Folks come to see the statue, and incidentally buy some peanuts.

"Well, where can we go now? I say to set out and have a look at the tower where she was imprisoned. Pulled down! It isn't, either;

it's starred in the book. What's that? This tower named for her, and hers pulled down! Well, there's French honor for you again. What do you think of Sibbilly now, Edna? I don't want to see the tower if it ain't the real one. I want to see the bas-reliefs of the Field of the Cloth of Gold, and then I want to go back to the hotel to lunch. I tell you, this sight-seeing is a great appetizer. The more old ruins and burnings I look over, the hungrier I get.

"Is this the place? Makes me think of a sort of glorified gate to a woodyard. What is it, now? Well, ask somebody! A bank, eh? Are those the famous bas-reliefs? Those! Them! Well, well, I must say the touring public is easy game. They're all worn off. What's the tin overhead for? To keep the rain from damaging them, eh? Pretty bit of sarcasm, eh, Bob? Great pity they didn't think to put it four or five hundred years sooner. I don't see a man with a head or a horse with a leg from here. It lacks character, to my idea. Let's go home. Come on. I've racked around Rouen all I care to for one day."

III

YVONNE TO HER MOTHER

Rouen.

Dearest Mama: It is midnight, and I must tell you the most astonishing piece of news. We came here with Uncle last night, and all this morning we were out with him. When we came home and unlocked our room we found *Lee* sitting by the window. But he doesn't want Uncle to know. It was fortunate that Uncle's room is across the hall, for I screamed. We couldn't see how he got in, but he says that he has bent a buttonhook so that he can travel all over Europe. It seems he never meant to go to Russia at all; but he doesn't want Uncle to know. He says he thinks Russia is a good place for Uncle to imagine him in. We had such fun! We told him all about the voyage and all about Uncle. He says M. Sibilet's mother *is* his wife—he married her for money. He says he's a painter. Lee is really going yachting, but he doesn't want Uncle to know. He isn't going for a while, though; and he doesn't want

Uncle to know that, either. While we were talking, Uncle rapped, and Lee had to get into the wardrobe while Uncle came in and read us a lecture. When we were in the cathedral to-day he found a man he used to know in school, and he was utterly overjoyed until he saw that the man had a son; and then, of course, he was worried over the son. So he came in to-night to tell us that it he discovered any skylarking, he should at once give up a friendship which had always meant more to him than we young things could possibly imagine. He said we must understand that he'd have no sort of foolishness going on, and at that the wardrobe creaked so awfully that Edna had a fit of coughing, and I didn't know what I should have if he kept on. He didn't go until it was high lunch-time, and I was afraid Lee would have to stay in the wardrobe until he smothered. When Uncle was gone, Edna asked Lee how under the sun he kept still, and he said he nearly died, because so many hooks hooked into his coat and he had nothing to perch on except shoe-trees. I do think Lee is so clever. I wish Uncle thought so, too. He went to his room, and we lunched with Uncle, Mr. Porter, and Mr. Porter, Jr.; and afterward we visited the church of the Bon-Secours and the monument to Jeanne d'Arc. She stands on top, her hands manacled, with her big, frightened eyes staring sadly and steadily out over the town where she met death. Uncle admired her so much that he tripped on one of the sheep that are carved on the steps, and after that he didn't admire anything or anybody. We got back about five, and Lee came in for a visit of an hour. Lee says he had a fine voyage. It stormed, and he says he never was battened down with such a lively lot of people. Uncle came in twice while he was there, but Lee has the wardrobe by heart now, and doesn't take a second. He says the men he's going yachting with are great sport, and he expects to have the time of his life. I do wish Uncle liked Lee, so that he could go around with us these days; he would be so much fun.

We are going to Jumièges to-morrow, Uncle says. Lee says he must take the early train for Havre. He's just been in to say good-by. He brought a cherry-tart and his shoe-horn, and we had ours, and so we had no trouble at all in eating it.

It has raised my spirits lots, seeing Lee. It seemed so terrible for him to go off to Russia like that. Uncle spoke of it yesterday. He said he was glad to have one worry off his mind and safe in Russia. The wardrobe squeaked merrily.

Now good-by.

Love from

Yvonne.

IV

YVONNE TO HER MOTHER

Rouen.

Dear Mama: Lee is gone. I do wish he could have stayed longer, but he thought it was risky. Uncle John was sure he smelt cigarette smoke in my room, and although it wasn't true at all, Edna cried and said the wardrobe was getting on her nerves, and Lee said he reckoned he'd take his button-hook and move on. We had an awful time bidding him good-by, for Uncle came in three times, and the second time he had lost his umbrella and thought it must be in our wardrobe. I never was so frightened in all my life; for, you know, if Uncle had been hunting for his umbrella and had found Lee, he wouldn't have liked it at all. Edna volunteered to look in the wardrobe, and I know I must have looked queer, for Uncle asked if I'd taken cold. You know how much I think of Lee, but I couldn't help being relieved when he was gone. It is such a responsibility to have a man in your wardrobe so much of the time. He said that I must try to steer Uncle toward Brittany, because he'll be yachting all around there. He says I must mark places in the Baedeker with strips of paper. He says that's a fine way to make any one go anywhere, and that if Edna and I will talk Italy and mark Brittany, Uncle is almost sure to wind up in the Isle of Jersey. Lee says he wishes he'd been kinder to Uncle in America, and then he'd like him better in Europe. He's afraid Uncle will never forgive him for taking him bobbing that time and dumping him off in the snow. It was too bad.

We went to Jumièges to-day. Uncle found it in the guide-book, and we took an eleven-o'clock train. Mr. Porter and his son were late, and just had time to get into the rear third-class coach. Uncle was much distressed until we came to Yainville, where the train stopped, and they got out. Uncle wanted them to get in with us, and he talked so forcibly on the subject that the train nearly started again before Mr. Porter could make him understand that Yainville is where you get off for Jumièges.

I do wish it wasn't so hard to turn Uncle's ideas another way when he's got them all wrong.

Yainville has a red-brick depot on the edge of a pleasant, rolling prairie, but there is a little green omnibus to hyphenate it with Jumièges. We were a very tight fit inside, for of course we could only sit in Uncle's lap, and he didn't suggest it, so I had to hold Edna; and Mr. Porter and his son knew Uncle well enough not to suggest taking her. I thought that we should never get there; and it was so tantalizing, for the country became beautiful, and we could only see it in little triangular bits between shoulders and hats. Young Mr. Porter wanted to get out and walk, but Uncle said, "Young man, when you are as old as I am, you will know as much as I do," so he gave up the idea. I do believe we were cooped up for a solid hour before we finally rolled down a little bit of a hill into a little bit of a village, and climbed stiffly out into the open air.

We all had to cry out with wonder and admiration then, it was really so wonderful. On one side were the hills, with the Seine winding off toward Paris; and on the other side was the wood, with the ragged ruins of the abbey-church walls towering up out of the loftiest foliage. Uncle thought we had better go and see all there was to be seen directly, so we walked off down the little road with a funny feeling of being partly present and partly past, but very well content.

The story goes that one of the ancient French kings took two young princes of a rival house, crippled them, put them on a boat, and set them afloat at Paris. They drifted down the current as far as this spot, and here they were rescued. They founded a monastery in gratitude, and their tomb was in the church, which is now in ruins. Later we saw the stone, with their effigies, in the little museum by the gate. They were called "Les Deux Enervés," in reference to their mutilation. Uncle thought the word meant "nervous," and we heard him say to Mr. Porter, "Well, who wouldn't have been, under the circumstances?" The whole of the abbey is now the private property of a lady who lives in a nice house up over back beyond somewhere. She built the lodge, and also a little museum for relics from the ruins, and has stopped the wholesale carrying off of stones from the beautiful remnants of what must have once been a truly superb monument. I am sure I shall never in all my life see anything more grand or impressive than the building as it is to-day. It is much the same plan as the cathedral at Rouen, only that that has been preserved, and this has been long abandoned. It is so curious to think of the choir which we saw yesterday, with its chapels and stained glass, and then to compare it with this roofless and windowless one, out of the tops of the walls of which fir-trees—big ones—are growing. You don't know what a strange sensation it is to see trees growing out of the tops of ruined walls the foundations of which were laid by Charlemagne's relatives. Edna and I felt very solemn, and Uncle was quiet ever so long, and then only said, "I vow!" The grass is growing in the nave and transept, and the big carved pediments stick up through the turf here and there, with moss and lichen clinging to the shadowy sides. The rows of pillars are pretty even, and the set of big arches above are mostly all there still. There were a third and a fourth gallery above, and although they are fallen away in places, still you can see exactly how it used to be. When you look away up to the fourth tier of columns, the main walls of the nave are still soaring higher yet; and when you follow the sky-line of their vastness, you see the two mighty towers rising, rising, straight up toward heaven, with the rooks whirling and circling about them and screaming in the oddest, most awfully mournful manner. I'm sure I shall never feel the same way again, not even if I live to be a thousand years old myself. I felt overcome; I felt a way that I never felt before. I don't know what I felt.

 Uncle was delighted; he sighed with satisfaction. "This is the real thing," he said to Mr. Porter; "I like this. You can see that there's been no tampering with *this* ruin." Mr. Porter looked up at the sky above and said: "I should say that there had been considerable tampering with this ruin. I will take my oath that the whole of the little town yonder was built with the stone taken from these walls and those of the monastery buildings."

"There's been no tampering with *this* ruin"

    Uncle is getting very nervous over Mr. Porter, Jr., because he walks around with Edna so much; so we were not allowed out of his sight during the visit, and didn't explore half as much as we wanted to. The little museum was really very interesting, and had the tombstone of one of Joan of Arc's judges. I feel very sorry for Joan's poor judges. They had to do as they were bid, and have been execrated for it ever since.

    We came home late in the afternoon, and Mr. Porter found a telegram calling him to Brussels on business, so he and his son said good-by hurriedly and took a half-past-six train. Uncle said at dinner that it was a strange thing to see how, after forty-five years of seeing the world, a man could still be the same as when one had to do all his sums for him at school. We absorbed this luminous proposition in silence, and then Uncle looked severely at Edna and said that at the rate that things were progressing he wouldn't have been surprised to have had a John Gilpin in the family any day. We were struck dumb at this threat or prophecy or whatever was intended, and went meekly to bed. Edna had a letter from Lee and I had one from Harry. Lee didn't dare write me and Harry didn't dare write Edna because of Uncle. But they each sent the other their love.

Uncle wants to go to Gisors to-morrow.

P. S. I must add a line to tell you that Mrs. Braytree and the four girls have arrived. They saw Uncle on the stairs coming up, and all came straight to our room. They landed yesterday, and had a real good passage, only Eunice fell out of the berth and sprained her wrist. She has it in a sling. They had a hard time arranging about the dog, as the hotel didn't want him in the rooms. He is one of those dogs that look scratchy and whiny at the first glance. Mrs. Braytree has lost her keys, so she sat with us while the hotel people got a man to open her trunks. She says she's in no hurry to unpack, for she had so many bottles she's almost positive one cork at least must have come out. They entirely forgot to bring any hairpins and suffered dreadfully on shipboard on that account. They had trouble with one of their port-holes too, and Mrs. Braytree and Uncle are both going to carry crowbars at sea hereafter.

They are going to stay here a week. It's so nice to meet some one from home!

Always yours lovingly,
Yvonne.

V

UNCLE JOHN EN ROUTE

Rouen.

"Come on, girls, this is quite an expedition. I vow I shook a little when Mrs. Braytree suggested coming, too. Seven women to one man would be too many for comfort as a general thing; but your Uncle John never shows the white feather, so I only drew the line at the dog. Why the devil five women want to travel with one dog and eight trunks I can't see; but if I was Mrs. Braytree, I'd probably know more about it. Curious little creature, the cross-eyed one, isn't she? And that Pauline—always wanting to be somewhere else. I told her pretty flatly at dinner that if she couldn't get any more fun out of Rouen than by wishing it was St. Augustine, she'd better have stayed in New York. Anything but these fault-finders.

"Well, ain't you ready? I've sent the luggage along, and it seems to me that we ought to be following its good example. Lord knows, two days is enough to waste in an old hole like Rouen; I was wondering last night what we ever came for. I never was so cold anywhere in my life, and sleeping on a slope with a pillow on your feet isn't my idea of comfort at night, anyhow. I don't understand the moral of the scheme, and the pillow keeps sliding, and I keep swearing, all night long. Also, I can't learn to appreciate the joy of standing on a piece of oil-cloth to wash. I must say that one needs to wear an overcoat and ear-muffs to wash here, anyhow. I was dancing under the bell-rope and ringing for hot water a good half-hour this morning. I'm going to write and have the asterisk subtracted from this hotel.

"Well, come on, if you're ready. Whose umbrella is that getting left by the door? Mine? I vow, I didn't remember putting it down. But no one can think of everything. Edna, is this soap yours? No? Well, I just asked. I seem to have left mine somewhere, and it's live and learn. Come on! come on!

"Good morning, Mrs. Braytree—Eunice—Emma—Pauline—Augusta. I reckon we'd better be hustling along pretty promptly. The train doesn't go until five minutes after the time, if we don't hurry. It's truly a pleasure having you join us, Mrs. Braytree. A little excursion like this makes such a pleasant break in the routine of sight-seeing, I think, and these quaint old—there, all get out now, I have the money. I'll take the tickets; we're all full-fare, aren't we? Or—how old is the little cross-eyed one? I *beg* your pardon, Mrs. Braytree, but I had to know in a hurry.

"There, come on! come on! Squeeze through. Se—ven women and one man. Hurry! we want a compartment, here—no, there. Run, Edna, and get ahead of that old lady; here's two umbrellas to throw crossways, and then you can tell her there's no room, and the law will uphold you. You look surprised, Mrs. Braytree, but I learned that little trick coming from Havre. I tell you, by the time I get to Paris I'll be on to every kind of game going. I learn fast—take to Europe as a duck takes to water, so to speak.

"Well, we're off for Gisors. Great pleasure to have you with us, Mrs. Braytree; no more work to steer seven—Good Lord! there aren't but six here! Who isn't here? Edna's gone! What is it, Yvonne? I sent her ahead, did I? Oh, so I did, so I did. And of course she is waiting for us. Poor child! I hope she's not worried. As soon as we get out of the tunnel I'll hang out of the window and holler to her. Very convenient method of talking to your friends aboard, Mrs. Braytree; only I should think a good many would lose their heads as a consequence. However, as the majority of the heads would be foreigners', I don't suppose it would matter much in the long run.

"Speaking of Gisors, Mrs. Braytree, it's really a very interesting place—according to the guide-book. As far as I'm personally concerned, I'd be willing to take the time to go there to learn how to pronounce it. The workings of the mind which laid out the way to speak French don't at all jibe with the workings of the mind which laid out the way to spell it—not according to my way of thinking. There's that place which we've just left, for instance,—'Ruin' as plain as the nose on your—on anybody's face,—and its own inhabitants can't see it—pronounce the R in a way that I should think would make their tongues feel furry, and then end up as if, on second thought, they wouldn't end at all.

"Yvonne, I wish you'd hang out and see if you see any of Edna hanging out. I declare, this is a very trying situation to be in. You don't know what a trip I had, Mrs. Braytree, trying to keep track of these girls; and since we landed—well, I just had to call a halt in Havre and come off alone. Curious place, Havre, don't you think? See any one you knew there? We—who did you say? Why, that can't be, he's in Russia. Yvonne, didn't that young reprobate write you he was going to Russia? Yes, I thought so. Well, Mrs. Braytree says she saw him in Havre. Good joke his not knowing we were in Rouen; he'd have been down there in a jiffy, I'll bet anything. But your Uncle John is a rather tough customer to handle, and I expect that young man knows the fact, and so thought it best to give Rouen a wide berth. Not that I have anything in particular against young Reynolds, only I don't consider that any girl could be happy with him. And it's foolish to have a man around unless you can make him happy—I mean unless he can make you happy. My wife was very happy up to the time she developed melancholia—a sad disease, Mrs. Braytree. Yvonne, I wish you'd hang out and see if you can see anything of Edna.

"I presume this is as good a time as we'll have to study up a little on Gisors. It seems to have been the capital of the Vexin. I shouldn't be surprised if 'vex' and 'vexing' both come from that country, for the guide-book gives it as always in hot water. The French and English were both up against it most of the time, and it was vexin' with a vengeance. It says here that the old city walls are still standing and that Henry II built the castle. Isn't he the one we peeked around in Rouen? Yes, I thought so. It says that there's very little left of the castle, though. I must say I'm always glad when I read that there's not much left of anything; it gives me a quiet, rested sort of feeling."

"'This is as good a time as we'll have to study up on Gisors'"

Gisors.

"Well, here we get out. I'll swing down first. If French trains were American, they'd have trapezes or elevators to—get—out—by. Here, give me your hand, Yvonne—oh, there's Edna. Well, I vow, who has she got—if it isn't—Yvonne, isn't that that young man— how d'ye do, Edgar? Delighted to see you again. Our friend, Mrs. Braytree, and all the others are her daughters. Come, Edna; you come with me while I check this trunk. Where in thunder did you get that fellow from? How does he come to be in Rouen? Did you know he was in Rouen? Did you see him while he was there? I declare, I never will travel with any women again unless I am married to them. This is awful. Don't you know I'm responsible for you two girls? And I send you ahead to get a compartment, and you find Edgar—it makes me want to swear. Say, was there any one else with you? Worse and worse. I was afraid there was something wrong when we kept hanging out and you never hung out at all. Well, we'll have to go back and gather them all up. Yes, I'll be polite to him; but, Edna, I hope you understand distinctly that a man like that could never make any woman—

"Yes, Mrs. Braytree, here we are again; and now we'll all proceed over Gisors. Pretty place, don't you think? Picturesque. Did you ever see so many canals—or smell so many?—and the little cottages out of another century? Packed roofs—green trees—well-sweeps—I like this; I'm glad I had the sense to come here. Edgar, will you oblige me by carrying that cane so that child doesn't come within an ace of catching her mouth on it every other second? I declare, Mrs. Braytree, I wish we hadn't run on to that young man. Of course he's a nice fellow and all that, but young men are a great trial when you have two—

"Let's turn down here. Most of the streets seem to be canal tow-paths. I vow, this *is* pretty. I could settle down in a place like this and live till I died. What do you suppose the people here do to amuse themselves, anyhow? From the way they look at us with their mouths open I should imagine that we were regarded in the light of a great event. And if that's the case, they must be pretty hard up for sport. Oh, well, I presume it's enough for them to paddle about on the green waters and stir up the miasma—as much sense as foreigners have.

"And so these are the walls—ramparts, I mean. Well, they're fairly high. Wonder how high they are, anyhow? Edgar, will you do me the courtesy not to be pointing to the left with that cane of yours when I turn suddenly to the right again? I beg your pardon for seeming heated, Mrs. Braytree; but he really—

"Let's find a gate and go in; seems to be a park inside. I should think there *was* 'little left to be seen of the castle!' I don't see anything at all of it. Maybe they took it down and built the walls higher just to fool tourists. Well, I didn't come to Gisors to caper about in a park; let's go out and look at the church—the guide-book says the church is worth seeing. I think there's something very touching about guide-book enthusiasm: it keeps up so consistently right through to the end. I feel as if my own enthusiasm was most run through now. I don't know how Paris will affect me. Edgar, if I trip on that cane you'll have to pay my doctor's bill. What makes you handle it as you do, anyway? I like to see a cane light and alert—not one that drags through the world in the style of yours. To judge from your cane, I should say you hadn't been in bed before three for a month. I have to speak sharply to that fellow, Mrs. Braytree; he is about as wooden-headed as they make. Came across the ocean with us, and pestered the life out of me. You don't know what an ocean voyage is with two attractive girls—I *beg* your pardon; I forgot your four. Dear me! we were speaking of—yes—of Gisors, of course. I vow, I'm disappointed in it as a whole. I wish we'd gone to Les Andelys instead. Les Andelys is marked with an asterisk in the guide-book, and there's a castle there built by Cœur-de-Lion. By the way, Mrs. Braytree, the Cœur-de-Lion *itself* is buried in Rouen. Did you know that? Nice joke, eh? But, dear, dear, if there's no castle here when we get here, perhaps there'd be none there when we got there. I'm beginning to look upon Europe as a confidence-game; I—

"Well is *that* the castle! Great Scott! but it must have been big. It's big yet, and the book said there was very little left to see. I'm beginning to lose faith in that book. Picturesque idea, having the park hide the ruins till you come right smash on to them. Clever people, the French; make everything put the best foot foremost. Fine old round tower; nice tumble-down guard-chamber! I like this. Let's go around the other side. Great place, eh? Worth a trip to see. Edgar, let me have your cane to point with. There, do you see that old staircase? Looks Roman to me; what do you think? I tell you, a man could write an historical novel out of old ruins if he prowled long enough. Come on now; let's meander on down town and look at the church. As soon as I look at anything, I'm always ready to look at something else. Let's go out on this side and go back to town the other way. Then we'll look at the church, and then we'll put you and Edgar on the train for Rouen, Mrs. Braytree. What did you say, Yvonne? He isn't going to Rouen? Where is he going? To Paris with us! Well, well, well! all I can say is, I do admire his nerve. I never in all my life went where I wasn't asked, and took a cane. Now don't you see why no woman could be happy with a man like that? I never saw the beat. I tell you frankly, Yvonne, I don't like his ways and I don't like him. If you girls had let him alone on the boat, he'd have let us alone here. I declare, my day is just about spoiled. Your mother has trusted you girls to me, and I haven't drawn a quiet breath since. I did take a little comfort there in Rouen; but if I'd known that Lee was in Havre, I'd have been on thorns even there.

"Well, where is the church? Ask some one. What did she say? Down here? Down we go, then. Ah, I suppose that's it under the sidewalk. Nice commanding situation for a church, to grade a street by its tower! Why don't they put in the guide-book, 'Street commands a fine view of the roof?' There isn't time to go inside unless Mrs. Braytree wants to miss her train, and we don't want her to do that.

"This is the street to the *gare*, and we'll run right along. I expect we can get something to eat there, and get that 1:30 train for Beauvais. There isn't anything in Beauvais that would interest you, Mrs. Braytree; but there's a church there that I want to see. The guide-book says that Mr. Ruskin says that the roof has got a clear vertical fall that not many rocks in the Alps can equal; I don't just know what a clear vertical fall may be, but if there's a church anywhere near as high as an Alp, I don't want to miss seeing it.

"There's the clock. You just have time to get aboard comfortably. Don't you want to go with them, Edgar? Well, I thought maybe you might. Good-by, good-by; delighted to have met you. Good-by. Oh, yes, of course. In Paris.

"There, they're gone, darn 'em! Now let's get some lunch. Did you ever see such a collection as those girls? It must have been a bitter pill when, after managing to assimilate the looks of the three oldest, the little one appeared with her eyes laid out bias. Come in here; we can get something to eat here, I don't care what; but I want plenty. Don't lose your cane, Edgar; life wouldn't be life to you without it, I expect. I like these country hotel entrances, through a carriage-house and a duck-yard, fall over a cat, and come in. Tell her we want dinner for four, and prompt. You put that in good forcible French for me, Edgar, and I'll be grateful to you till I die. Let's sit down. Let's eat."

"'Tell her we want dinner for four, and prompt'"

Beauvais.

"Now, young people, I call this making a day count. This is my idea of getting about. Breakfast in Rouen, lunch in Gisors, Beauvais for a sandwich, and we'll dine in Paris.

"What time is it? Three o'clock. Well, we want to head straight for that cathedral. Seems as if it ought to show most anywhere over a little, low town like this, but I don't see it. Ask someone—ask any one. Well, what did they say? Right across the square. Whose statue is that in the middle? Joan of Arc? Jeanne Hachette? Who was Jeanne Hachette? Girl who captured flag from Charles the Bold, eh? Is that why they called him 'the Bold'? Sort of sarcastic on his letting a girl carry off his flag, I should consider. Well, when did she live? Has she got her year under her? 1492. Seventy years after Joan. I shouldn't have thought she'd have inspired other young women in this part of the country to emulate her.

"Do we go up here? Ugh, how I hate walking over cobble-stones! Clean; of course they're clean. I didn't say that I thought they were dirty. I said I hated to walk on 'em.

"What's that chopped-off creation before us? *Not* the cathedral? Well—I—vow!

Beauvais

"Is *that* what I—what we—

"Where's the front of it? What *did* happen to it? And what *was* Mr. Ruskin thinking of when he compared it to an Alp! I don't want to fall off of anywhere, but I'd choose the roof of that cathedral to start from any day in preference to the lowest Alp they make. 'Clear vertical fall' eh? I wish I knew what that meant.

"Well, let's go in. Where's the door? That little, unpretentious one looks feasible. Come on. Well, Edgar, are you coming, too, or do you choose to stay outside with your stick? I can't help it, Edna; I feel irritated at his being here at all, and then I'm naturally disappointed over this church. I must say the biggest thing about it is that blank wall stopping up where they left off. This is the kind of thing I've come several thousand miles to look at, is it? Well, may as well go in, I suppose.

"So this is in the inside! Fine lot of carpets hung up to try and cover the deficiencies, eh?—High roof,—funny sort of shock you get whenever you look towards the front. Sort of like turning around and hitting your cane, eh, Edgar? Girls, this cathedral was begun in 1180, time of Henry II, and they quit in 1555 while Bloody Mary was abroad and never got to the front end in the four hundred years. Well, well! dear, dear!

"'What's that chopped-off creation before us?'"

"Come on, girls, we may as well go out; I feel like going to the station and heading for Paris. I suppose that's the next move in the game. You can stay here as long as you like, Edgar; we won't hurry you.

"Come, Yvonne, you walk with me. Did you ever see anything like that young man's gall? Your friend Lee couldn't make any points around him. Just hooks right on to us, and stays hooked. I declare, if I carried a cane I bet I'd give him one punch he'd remember long after. I'd sincerely beg his pardon. I didn't like him on the steamer; I've got no use for young men of his stamp. I—"

Gare du Nord, Paris.

"So this is Paris! Now, Edgar, I have one favor to ask of you—will you kindly allow me to manage my own affairs while you manage yours? I know just what to do, and I'll take Yvonne with me to do it. You can take Edna up to the hotel. Looked disappointed, didn't he? Counting on endearing himself to me forever by his able-bodied assistance, I'll wager; but I don't want any young man minding my business. Tell that blue blouse to take these checks and look up five trunks in a hurry. What did he say? We haven't got to overhaul them again here, have we? Well, I am—I certainly just *am*. Have we got to hunt 'em up? Where? Well, ask him? Round back of this crazy mob? Well, tell him to go first. What's this system of wildly speculating wheat-pits? Baggage-counters, eh? And will you look at the baggage! Talk about your 'clear vertical falls!' Those trunks on top will soon know more than Ruskin ever did.

"Where's our man gone? Yvonne, do you know where that fellow went to? Well, ask some one. Look out—that baggage truck will be Juggernauting right over you before you know it. Now, where *is* the porter? I call this a pretty state of affairs—porter, valises, and trunk-checks all gone together. I thought you were watching him or I would have done so. Do you suppose we ought to speak to a policeman? I think we ought to. But will you look at the trunk-unlocking that's going on—good as a play—look how mad that old lady is; hear her give it to him in good English. Guess something got broke in transit. Keep a sharp eye out for that porter, Yvonne. Here come some more trunks, and more, and more yet. I wonder if this is regular, or if we've struck a rush. Where *is* that porter? I think we ought to be speaking to a policeman, don't you? Here's a choice new invoice of a couple of thousand more trunks; that fellow will never be able to find ours, I know. Supposing he has found them and gone off with them already. Hey, look at that lady jumping up and down! She sees *her* trunk, I'll bet a dollar. Well, I'd jump up and down if I could see mine. Yvonne, I really think we ought to speak to a policeman. Could you give a description of the man? I only remember that he wore a blue blouse. Oh, yes; and he had 'Commissionaire' across the front of his cap. Hello, here are nine trucks all at once, just a few million more additions to the turmoil. I tell you, we won't get out of here to-night, I don't believe. I vow, I wish I'd given the checks to Edgar, as he suggested. I really think we ought to be calling a policeman. Here are fourteen trucks all loaded to the gunwales, and two mass-meetings and one convention of tourists all at once. Yvonne, this is beginning to look serious to me; I think that really we ought to call—

"'Look how mad that old lady is'"

"Oh, there he is with the whole of the stuff on one truck. Good idea; smart chap; and he wasn't so very long either, considering."

VI

YVONNE TO HER MOTHER

Paris.

Dearest Mama: Well we *are* arrived! It *is* Paris at last! But I thought we should surely die in transit. I don't know what Uncle would have said if he had known that Lee was in Rouen; he was dreadfully upset over Mrs. Braytree's telling him that she saw Lee in Havre. He was very unreasonable, and laid it up against Lee that Mrs. Braytree saw him. Just as if Lee could help it.

We had a pretty good time coming down, only Mr. Edgar came up and came down with us, and of course Uncle did not like that. I think that Mr. Edgar came up to come down with me because we had a lovely time on the steamer coming over together, but Uncle hardly gave me a chance to speak to him. Uncle seems just instinctively to know whom Edna and I want to talk to, and then won't let us. But of course I'm not complaining, for it was lovely of him to give us this trip, and we're enjoying every minute.

We arrived last night, and the only drawback is that Mrs. Clary isn't here. She left a note, and M. Sibilet's wife *is* his mother, and has a place out at Neuilly, and they were invited there for three days. She will be back to-morrow, and she left word for us to go straight to the Bon Marché and look at the white suits; so we did so. We told Uncle it was all right for us to go alone, and he had just gotten his mail, so he only said "Hum!" and we went. Just as we were taking the cab, who should we see but Mr. Chopstone. It was so lovely to see him again, and he got into the cab and went with us. We went to the Bon Marché, but it wasn't much fun with a man, so we came out after a little, and he proposed taking the Subway and going to the Trocadero. Just then we met a man that Mr. Chopstone knew, and he had red hair and eye-glasses. Mr. Chopstone introduced him, and invited him to go along; but he said it was no use, because it was the wrong day and we couldn't get in when we got there. By this time we were down in the Subway, and Mr. Chopstone suggested that we go to the Bois, so as not to have to go back up the stairs again. While we were talking, the train came and went in a terrible hurry, and we got aboard in between. After we were off, we found that Mr. Chopstone wasn't on. We didn't know what to do, because, of course, it was he that we knew, and not the red-haired man. The red-haired man said he would do whatever we pleased, and Edna thought we had better get right off; but I thought we ought to go right on. We didn't know *what* to do, and so we kept on to the Bois.

The Bois was just lovely—all automobiles and babies; and who do you think we met? Betty Burleigh. We were so surprised, for I thought she was in California for her lungs; but it seems that she's been in Dresden for her music all winter, and now she's here for her clothes. She was with an elderly French lady, and I don't think that the elderly French lady liked to have her stop and talk to us. I thought at first that perhaps it wasn't proper on account of the red-haired man, but in a second I saw the real reason. Betty glanced around and said, "Oh, Madame, où est Fakir?" Whereupon the elderly French lady looked absolutely terrified and tore madly off. We had quite a long talk before she came back with the most awful little black dog, which they evidently had *no* string to. She put him down and began to look displeased again, and Betty just glanced about and said calmly, "Oh, Madame, où es Fakir?" He had absolutely vanished again, and the elderly French lady sort of threw up her eyes and rushed wildly away. The red-haired man said, "Why don't you buy a chain for him?" Betty shrugged the Frenchiest kind of a shrug and said, "I don't have to chase him." The red-haired man said, "I should think she would buy the chain then!" and Betty shrugged a much Frenchier shrug, and said: "I wouldn't allow it. While she is running after him I can do as I please." The red-haired man laughed. Poor madame came panting up with the creature just then, and Betty said sweetly, "Laissez-lui courir," so she had to put him down; but I could see that she meant to keep a sharp eye on him. Betty wanted us all to come to the Palais and lunch with her; but of course we refused, because you wouldn't have liked it, and, anyway, we had to go back to Uncle. She wanted the red-haired man to stay, anyhow, and was quite put out when he declined. Just then two men in an automobile came up and asked her to go and see the balloon ascension. They didn't invite the elderly French lady, and she protested about "comme il faut"—but Betty said, "Où est Fakir?" and, if you'll believe me, that little beast was gone again, and poor madame dashed off in

Seeing France with Uncle John

pursuit. Betty made short work of bidding us good-by then, and at once got into the automobile, and was off.

We came slowly along back with the red-haired man, and at the Arc de Triomphe we ran into Mr. Chopstone. It seems he went a station too far because he met some people he knew in the car behind us, and he says we must all go to the Châtelet with him tonight to make up. He said "Uncle, too," so we accepted. Then we took a cab and came back to the hotel, where we found our beloved relative with his feet on the center-table, reading the Paris "Herald." He looked over the top at us and announced that he'd "done the Louvre." I think we must have looked startled, for he went on to say at once that he knew that it was something that had got to be done, and that he shouldn't enjoy, and so he had thought it best to go at it the first thing on the first morning and get it off his mind at once. He was very pleased with himself, because he says the "Baedeker" says that it takes two hours and a half to walk through, and he was only gone from the hotel two hours in all. Edna asked him if he spent much time looking at the pictures, and he said: "Young lady, if you'd ever been in the place, you'd never ask that question. Why, the whole thing is lined with pictures. I bet I dream of gilt frames for a week."

We found our beloved relative

We had to go to lunch, and Uncle doesn't like the food very much; he says it strikes him as "flummery," and he is really very much vexed over Mrs. Clary's being at Neuilly. Edna is vexed because Harry is there, too, and I'm very much vexed indeed because she thoughtlessly gave Uncle the letter at lunch, and when he read about Monsieur Sibilet's wife being his mother he was more put out than ever. He said we could look out for ourselves this afternoon, as he had to go to the bank. Edna suggested that we go to the Louvre, and he said yes, that would be wise, because then we would all be free to enjoy ourselves. Uncle speaks of the Louvre exactly as if it were the semiannual siege at the dentist's. But he was kind enough to offer to leave us there on his way to the bank, and when we took the cab, he arranged with the cabman and the hotel-porter exactly what the fare was to be, and held it in his hand the whole way.

  Edna and I were mighty glad to get to the Louvre without Uncle, especially with the way he feels to-day, and we were wandering along in a speechless sort of ecstacy when all of a sudden I heard some one calling my name. I whirled around, and if it wasn't Mrs. Merrilegs, in a state of collapse on one of the red-velvet benches. We went to her, and she took hold of our hands as if she'd been our long-lost mother for years. She looked very white and tired and almost ready to faint, and we sat down on each side of her in real sincere sympathy, and she held our hands and told us how it was. It seems that they left home the last of last month, and they've been all through the British Isles, Denmark, Holland, and Belgium, and they are going to finish Europe and be home the first of next month. She could hardly speak for tears. She says Mr. Merrilegs made out the itinerary before they sailed and that they have lived up to it every day except just one, when he ate some lobster crossing the Irish Sea, and they lost a day that night. She says they drive a great deal, because they can hardly walk any more, and that she doesn't believe that there will be a museum or palace in Europe that they won't be able to say that they have driven by when they go home. She said they had come to the Louvre to see what pictures they wanted for their new house, and that they never meant to take more than twenty minutes for the selection, and that they had been there an hour already. She felt badly because the itinerary had them visit Notre Dame, the Eiffel Tower as high as the elevator goes, and Versailles this afternoon. She said they wanted to try and call on the American consul, too, to ask about a masseur. She said Mr. Merrilegs said he thought if they could get hold of a good masseur and keep him right with them that they could manage to rub through to the end.

"She took our hands as if she'd been our long lost mother for years"

Edna and I felt dreadfully sorry for her; but there did not seem to be anything to do except look sad, and we did that as heartily as we knew how until in a minute or two Mr. Merrilegs hove in sight with a funny little Frenchman dancing round and round him. Mr. Merrilegs looked almost as exhausted as his wife, and called Edna by my name and me by hers. His wife asked him if he had ordered the pictures, and he said: "No; I haven't any more time to waste here. I've given Claretie the paper with the sizes of the spaces marked on it, and he's to go through and measure till he finds a famous picture to match each space." Mrs. Merrilegs sort of nodded faintly and said: "But we don't want any martyrs in the dining-room, you know," and her husband said, "Yes, yes, he understands; and he says he'll find a Susanna to fit your bath, too." Mrs. Merrilegs stood up then with a very audible groan, and they both shook hands with us in a way that quite wrung our hearts. Then they limped away with the little Frenchman spinning gaily about them, and we went on alone.

In the very next room we met Mr. Chopstone. He was awfully glad to see us, and said, with our permission, he'd join us; but as he seemed joined anyway, we didn't even dream of refusing. He asked if we'd told Uncle about the Châtelet, and then we remembered that we had forgotten. He said he was so glad, because he couldn't get any seats except *baignoirs*, and they looked queer, because no one can see you. He asked if we would like to go to the opera instead, and we were just discussing it when we turned a corner and ran right on to Betty Burleigh and the red-haired man. His name is Potter, and, did you ever! They looked so upset that it can't have been an accident, their being together. But how could they have arranged it? If they didn't arrange it, why did they look upset? Betty had on a bright green cloth dress and a violet hat, and the red-haired man heightened the general effect so much that we moved on as quickly as possible. Mr. Chopstone said very roundly: "You'd better fight shy of her, I think," and Edna said dryly: "Of him, too, don't you think?" I waited a minute, and then I said it seemed droll to think that if we were all English we'd be pleased to call poor Betty a typical American.

We came home when the Louvre closed and found Uncle back with his feet on the center-table. He had had a big fire built, for he said it gave him chills to look at the nymph over his bed. He had put in a true Merrilegian afternoon, having been to the Palais de Justice, Sainte-Chapelle, Notre Dame, and driven by the Hôtel de Ville and around the Opera House—"completely around." He says there won't be a thing left for him to look at by Monday. He says if he was pressed for time he'd hire a cab for one whole day and lump the business; but that, seeing that we have the time, it really doesn't seem necessary.

The mail came while we were talking, and the most unfortunate thing happened. To keep up the Russian idea, Lee wrote two postals and sent them to St. Petersburg to be mailed. Uncle saw the Russian stamps and knew Lee's writing, and he asked me to kindly tell him how Mrs. Braytree came to see a man who was in Russia in Havre. Edna said weakly that it must have been a joke, and Uncle shook his watch and held it to his ear that way he always does when he's dangerous, and said he was in no mood for any of Lee's jokes. He looked very severely at me and said that Lee was a scalawag, and that I ought to be ashamed of myself for having him around.

Mrs. Clary will be back to-morrow, and we're very glad, for Uncle is awful peppery and tartary, and says "Hum!" when we least expect it. Edna sent Mr. Chopstone a *petit-bleu*, asking him please not to ask us to go anywhere to-night. Mr. Edgar sent me some violets, but I had time to give them to the chambermaid before Uncle came in. If I only get a chance, I shall ask Mrs. Clary to declare that M. Sibilet's mother *is* his wife, even if she knows it's a lie. It doesn't seem possible that Uncle could really care for Mrs. Clary; but he's so cross if she talks to any one else that I almost wonder if he doesn't. Edna is all tired out, and says she will cry if Uncle tells her again that any man isn't the man to make any girl happy. She says she likes men, and she thinks that they all make her happy. She wanted to go to the Châtelet in a *baignoir*, and she was wild to go to the opera in anything.

We talk Italy and mark Brittany every chance we get, but Uncle says "Hum!" to Italy the same as he does to everything else these days. I'm sure I don't see what we'll do if he takes the rest of Europe as hard as he does this much. But of course I don't mean that we're not having a lovely time, and we never forget for a minute how kind he was to bring us.

Next day.

Oh, it has been awful! How can I write it all!

You see, Uncle has a little balcony, and the sun came out, so he did, too, this morning, on his little balcony. And he saw Mrs. Clary being brought back in an automobile by M. Sibilet and two French officers. Of course Harry was there, too, but that didn't mend matters any. In looking over, Uncle's glasses fell to the ground, and they were his comfortable ones with the rubber round the nose, and that part broke, too. Edna was taking a bath, and I had to stand the brunt of the whole. Uncle told me not to dare to fancy for a minute that he cared who Mrs. Clary went about with; but he did wish for the credit of America that she would steer clear of men like Sibilet. He was much put out over the French officers, too, and said that if he was a French officer he'd go and walk around Alsace until he came to his senses. While he was talking he knocked the water-pitcher over, and then Edna was ready to dress; so he went away while I sopped up the floor.

Mrs. Clary came in right afterward. She has had a splendid time, and she says she doesn't care what relation the old lady is so long as she can have them for friends. She has had no end of fun since she came from Havre, and she says it's a shame about Uncle. She went to a beautiful lawn-fête at a countess's, and she says I mustn't worry over Lee and Uncle. She rode horseback, too, and drove with a coach, and she says Edna must remember that Uncle is always peculiar and doesn't mean half he says. She went to two dinner-parties, and no one would believe that she was Harry's mother. She says I ought not to be exasperated over anything, because nothing in the world can be so exasperating as having a son with a moustache when you don't look thirty-five, and that she doesn't let *that* worry *her*. M. Sibilet is going to give a dinner for her at the Ritz, and she's going to get a lace dress all in one piece, and she says it was she who told Mr. Edgar that we were coming from Rouen, and that Betty Burleigh is considered very fast, and that it won't take long for her to settle Uncle. I'm sure I hope so with all my heart; but I don't believe he'll like the idea of the dinner-party much. Mrs. Clary says Mme. Sibilet's château is a perfect castle, and that one of the French officers in the automobile was a duke. She says we must be patient, and Uncle will get used to the Continent, just as all American men do. She says they never take to it like women, though. The other French officer was in the ministry once, and counts more than any duke. Mrs. Clary is always so sweet and comforting, and she is such a nice chaperon, because she always has men enough herself never to be spiteful.

Mr. Chopstone sent Edna back a *petit-bleu* that he had the box at the opera, and what should he do about it. Mrs. Clary says for us to go. She says she'll take care of Uncle, for she wants to straighten out her accounts, and she can just as well straighten him out at the same time. She gave me a long letter from Lee that he left with her, and she told Edna to go and have a nice walk with Harry, and she'd tell Uncle they were both asleep in their rooms. I declare, it's good to have her back. I feel as if a mountain was lifted off me, and on to her. She says you never dreamed of such fun as she's had out there at Neuilly, and that it's quite absurd—my worrying over little things like Lee and Uncle.

She talked so much that I grew quite light-hearted, and had early dinner and went off to the—

I'll have to write the rest to-morrow. A boy says Uncle wants to speak to me.

Next day.

I do believe Lee knows better how to manage Uncle than all of us put together!

When Uncle sent for me, I saw right off that Mrs. Clary hadn't gotten him anywhere near all smoothed out. He looked awfully vexed, and he told me he was done with Paris and he was going to clear out at once. He said he knew that Edna and I wanted to go to Italy, but, unfortunately, he couldn't see it himself in that light. Then he paused and said "Hum!" and I waited. After a little he said that he'd happened to run across two or three things lately that had rather interested him in Brittany, and how would I like to go there. I was almost stunned at the success of Lee's scheme, and I was so happy that I suddenly felt as if I wanted Mrs. Clary and Edna to be happy, too, and I threw my arms right around his neck and said: "Oh, *Uncle*, let's go off together—just you and me—and have a real good time together, all by ourselves. Will you?"

I must have done it *very* well, for Uncle's face smoothed out at once, and he told me that he'd been meaning to give me Aunt Jane's watch ever since she died, only that it needed a new spring, and he never could remember to take it to the jeweler's. His face clouded some later, and he shook his head and said he wished he felt more security as to Mrs. Clary and Edna; but then he crossed his legs the other way, and said we only had one life to live, and could I be ready to start by day after to-morrow. I said that I was sure I could, and he said "Hum!" very pleasantly, and I went to my own room and told Mrs. Clary. She was so pleased; she says I am a saint, and that it's too bad for me to miss the dinner. She is going to wear her pink pearls, and she says that she will try to telegraph Lee.

I will confess that my heart sinks a little bit from time to time when I think of trying to bear Uncle all alone for I don't know how long; but I have great faith in Lee, and I know that he'll be somewhere along the coast, and that will be a comfort.

Uncle has been out and bought a Gaelic grammar and the history of the Siege of La Rochelle, for he says he wants to have some intelligent conception of what he sees. He wants me to learn the grammar, and he says, where he sees to everything, he should think I could do a little trifle like that for him once in a while. When he put it that way, I thought I must try; but, oh, heavens! you ought to see that grammar!

I will write again as soon as I can. Harry is going to take us all to the Café aux Fleurs for tea.

Lovingly,
Yvonne.

VII

My Dearest Mama: We are *en route*! We left Paris at the cheerful hour of 7 a.m. yesterday morning. No one was up, and there was another train at half-past nine, but Uncle said that, considering the work that lay before us, we had better not begin by dawdling. I do think there is a happy medium between rising at five and "dawdling," but of course I didn't tell him so.

Edna sat up in bed and kissed me good-by. She and Mrs. Clary looked upon me as a cross between the saver of the situation, and a burnt offering on Uncle's altar; but they were all happy, and I didn't care—much.

Uncle mapped out the route, and, as a result, we got down at Chartres about half-past nine. He put the baggage in *consigne*, and then looked about with the air of a charger who sniffs the battle afar. I stood beside him, feeling like Mazeppa just before they let the horse loose.

The outlook from the station is not very attractive, and the first thing that Uncle said was that he didn't believe it was worth while stopping at all, and that he had a good mind to go on with the train; but just at that instant the train went on by itself, so we did not need to discuss the subject.

You see there is a high ridge that runs in front of the station, and Chartres is on the other side. Nearly all the towns here seem to be quite a little ways from the railway stations. Mr. Edgar says it's because the railroads run after their passengers in Europe instead of running over them, as they do in America. Uncle says it's very inconvenient, anyhow, and he pulled his hat down hard and said, "Well, let's have a look at the cathedral, anyway."

So we stormed the ridge forthwith, and spread down into the flat country beyond. As we descended the slope, Uncle began to be glad he had come. Chartres is very modest and mainly one story high, so the Cathedral towers aloft in a most soul-satisfying manner. Uncle said it was "Something like." I was ever so glad that he felt so because he said in Beauvais that something he had read had led him to expect that the cathedral there would be big enough to hold the Bartholdi Statue of Liberty in one of its niches, and of course he was horribly disappointed, as a consequence.

We walked straight to the cathedral, and it was so big that Uncle thought we had better each take one side and meet behind, "so as to save time and not miss anything." I acquiesced, because I mean to keep him good-tempered, if keeping good-tempered myself and acquiescing will do so.

We started "fair" in front of the middle front door, and I could hardly keep a straight face as we walked promptly and solemnly off in opposite directions. The cathedral is enormous and just covered with carving, and I was only part way down the side when I saw Uncle coming around the corner, swinging his umbrella in the briskest sort of manner. He looked absolutely disgusted when he saw me, and said in the most injured tone imaginable, "You must have been stopping to look!"

He wouldn't hear to my continuing my tour of circumnavigation, so we went inside at once, and there I held the guide-book and read the explanation while he kept up a running contradiction of everything I read. I don't see the good of Uncle's carrying a guide-book, for he says they needn't suppose he doesn't know better than most of it.

There is a wonderful carved marble screen around the altar, and a sacred statue with a yellow satin dress on; but being inside made Uncle want to be outside right away, so we left very quickly, and then he studied the Baedeker just long enough to let me notice how all the Roman noses on the kings and saints outside had been turned into Eskimo noses by the rains of centuries; and then he suddenly shut it, and said we would go right straight off then and there and see the famous enamels that Diane de Poitiers gave Henry II. He explained to me that this wasn't the English Henry II, but the French Henry II, and then he asked me which of us had the luggage-checks, and if I had noticed whether the train went at eleven or half-past. I must say it is like doing multiplications in your head to travel with Uncle, but of course I enjoy it, and the walk to St. Peter's Church was very pleasant, through quaint streets and along by little canals like those at Gisors.

The church was open, and open in more ways than one, for they were tearing up the whole floor to put in a furnace and gravestones and pick-axes were leaning up against the columns everywhere. There wasn't a soul to be seen, and Uncle was so happy to be able to poke about unconcierged for a while that I sat down and let him desecrate around with his cane until he came to with a start and asked me what I supposed we came to Chartres for, anyway. I got up at that, and we went to look at the enamels, which are in behind a locked balustrade and have curtains hung in front of them besides. We had to get a woman to unlock the gate and draw the curtains aside and explain which enamel was which Apostle; and uncle was very much put out over their being apostles at all. I don't know what he expected in a church, but he said he never thought about the church; he only thought about Diane de Poitiers. He says he doesn't think it was in good taste her having anything to do with the apostles, and then he read in the book again and found he'd made a mistake, and it was the king who gave them to her, and not she who gave them to the king, and that used him all up, and he said he wished that he had never come.

I saw that we should have to have something to eat right off, so I said I was hungry and Uncle said that was just like a woman, but to come on. We found a small restaurant and had a very good lunch, and then Uncle said if I felt satisfied he would take it as a personal favor if we could go on to Dreux. I do wish he wouldn't put everything just that way when I really haven't done anything; but he looked at his watch and found that the time before when he had looked at it he had looked at it wrong and that we had barely ten minutes to make the train. As a matter of fact, the train was going then, but they don't go until ten minutes after in France, so when you miss a train you always have ten minutes left to make it. We took a cab, and Uncle made the man understand that if he hurried it would pay; so we galloped madly over the ridge and just got aboard in time to learn that Uncle had left his cane in the cab and that we'd forgotten our luggage in *consigne.*

   Of course the ride was rather gloomy, because there was almost no way to lay the blame on me; but after a while Uncle asked me if I really ever did see such a rank idiot as M. Sibilet, and he felt better after that. We reached Dreux about two o'clock, and I telegraphed back about the luggage while Uncle looked up a train for Argentan and set his watch by the railway time. He told me that the train that he had decided on left at 3:04 and that we could make it and see the mausoleum "easy." I never contradict Uncle, because it doesn't do any good and does upset him awfully, so I went with him to get the cab, and wondered how long a mausoleum usually took to examine.

Dreux

It seems that there are no cabs in Dreux!

I thought that that would end the mausoleum, but Uncle merely swept his eyes over the prospect and said we'd have to walk, and walk pretty prompt. It was 2:10, and we walked fast. The mausoleum is on top of a hill, and Uncle said we could catch our breath after we got to the top. We never spoke a word going up. I knew that I was too young to die of heart-disease, so I didn't care, if he didn't.

It was a terrible climb, but we reached there at 2:32. It's the mausoleum of the Orléans family, and is modern. There is a concierge who takes you around, and we followed him, Uncle with his watch in his hand and going on like this: "2:40—tomb of the king's mother, eh? Fine old lady! 2:41—tomb of the Duc d'Aumale; good face, handsome decorations on his bosom, stained-glass windows—all made at Sévres, eh? 2:43—" etc. You can imagine!

But what you can't imagine is the sublime and peaceful beauty of all those exquisite marble people sleeping there under the slanting rainbow sun-rays of the magnificent windows. They affected me so deeply that, in spite of Uncle, I could hardly keep back the tears. They didn't seem living and they didn't seem dead; I don't know what they were like—spirits made visible, perhaps. The Duchesse d'Orléans has her arm stretched across, so that it touches her husband, who was the eldest son of Louis Philippe. The king himself stands upright in the midst of them all, and Queen Marie Amélie kneels at his side in a beautiful pose. Two precious little babies are sculptured together on one tomb, and all the while we were going about, the place resounded with the echoes of the chisels that were preparing a place for the Prince Henry who was killed in Africa.

I could have stayed there hours, wrapped up in the mystery and wonder of it all, but Uncle fell down some steps while he was looking at his watch, and we departed forthwith. He said we must walk fast, and so again we walked fast. Of course it was easier, though, going down-hill, and I said, when we were near enough not to be anxious any more, "It was worth seeing, wasn't it?" To which Uncle replied: "Yes, if you enjoy that kind of thing; but all I could think of was the idea of spending such a lot of money on statues and then not having any cabs at the depot."

There was no time to get anything more to eat at the moment, so I just held my tongue until we were safely on the train again.

We reached Argentan at 6:15 p.m., and I felt as if I'd been running Uncle, or, rather, running with Uncle, for a month.

The next morning we were called at seven, and I really thought that I could not get up at first; but, I made it at the third try, and Uncle and I were out "seeing Argentan" at eight. At half-past he declared that there was really nothing to see, so we went to the *gare*, and he bought a Paris "Herald." As we were sitting there waiting for the 8:04 train to Coulibœuf, in came Elfrida Sanders and her sister with bicycles. I was *so* astonished, and Uncle was rather pleased, too. They are doing Normandy on wheels, and they have their tools and a kodak and a small set of toilet-things and four clean collars all tied on to them. Elfrida says they've had a lovely time—only broken glass once, and rain two days. The sister is going to write a book and call it "Two on a Trot." I think that's a funny name for a bicycle story. Uncle said to call it "Two on a Tire"; but you know how stupid Elfrida is, and so she said, "Oh, but it's not a tandem." They were going to Coulibœuf, too, but we couldn't go together because they were traveling third-class. Elfrida says they are seeing Europe nicely on less than a dollar a day, and Uncle said "Great Scott!"

"Elfrida says they are seeing Europe nicely on less than a dollar a day, and Uncle said 'Great Scott!'"

While we were on the train it began to rain and then it poured. Uncle became very gloomy and said that is just what we might have expected. I didn't expect rain, and I didn't see why I should have expected it, so I only nodded. Uncle didn't like my nodding, and said I shouldn't take such a pessimistic view of life at my age. While he was talking I suddenly remembered the umbrella and asked him where it was, and he had left it in Argentan! Then there was no more conversation.

Falaise

We had to change cars at Coulibœuf, and we reached Falaise about noon. Elfrida and her sister got right on to their wheels and bumped gaily away over the cobblestones at once. The rain was over and the sun was shining, but Uncle said he had lost all faith in France and wanted to buy another umbrella the very first thing. We went to a store, and he said to buy a cheap one, as I would be sure to lose it. I asked for a cheap one, but the woman was quite indignant and said that she did not keep any cheap umbrellas—that the lowest she had was two francs—forty cents. I had to translate it to Uncle, and he was so amused that he bought one for three francs and gave a franc to her baby that was tied in a high chair by the window.

Then we took a cab to the castle and paid the man at the entrance and let him go. There is a lovely sloping road that follows the curve of the outer wall up to the summit of the hill, and we forgot how tired we were in thinking how pretty it was. These old castle enclosures are all so big. This one contains a college at one end, and then there is quite a wood which you must walk through before you come to the castle itself at the other end.

The castle is wonderful. It is splendid and big and old and strong and Norman. It is built out of the red rock, and it has oubliettes and wells and pits and towers and everything of the kind that heart could wish to see. We saw the room where Prince Arthur was imprisoned for seven years and the room where William the Conqueror was born. It's a very little room in which to have had such a wonderful thing happen.

"Paid the man at the entrance and let him go."

Uncle enjoyed the castle immensely; he took the deepest interest in every inch of it, and when the concierge showed us the window from which Robert the Devil first saw Arlette, he planted himself firmly inside it and I almost thought that he was going to stay there forever. My feet ached so that I was glad enough to lean up anywhere for a minute, and I honestly believe that it was ten before he moved. Then he gave himself a little shake and said: "Well to think of owning this place, and being able to stand in a window as high up as that one, and then to look down as far as that well is, and then only to need to say, 'Bring her up!' and to know she'd got to come! Great Scott! No wonder their son conquered England. I'm only surprised that he didn't wipe Europe off the face of the continent!" Then he shook his head for quite a little while, and we got under way again and went to Talbot's Tower.

"The coming down was awful"

It's high, and Uncle wanted to climb it. I didn't mind his climbing it, but he wanted me to climb it, too, and some one was ringing the bell, so the concierge had to leave us and go back before anything was settled. Uncle said it was rather hard when he was doing so much to try and finish me up (he meant "finish me off," I think), for me to be so lukewarm about being finished so I started in to climb, although my knees felt like crumpled tissue-paper. The steps were so worn that it was awful work and Uncle would go up as far as anyone could. He had the umbrella and I had the candle and often we had to step two and even three steps at once. When we came to the place where the steps ended, he stood and peeked out of a window (imagining himself Lord Talbot, I reckon—) and then we started back. The coming down was awful,—I was honestly frightened. Uncle went first and I stepped on his coat twice and spilt candle-grease on his hat. Uncle found it easier coming down than going up, and it wasn't until we reached the bottom that we discovered that the reason why was because he had left the umbrella behind and so had two hands to hold on by. I said, "Never mind, it only cost sixty cents"; but he was not to be comforted, and said bitterly, "You forget the franc that I gave her baby." I would have gone back for it, but I felt so hot and tired.

We came to Caen this noon, and went to bed, and I don't believe we shall ever get up again. Uncle said that with my kind permission he would suggest that I should not disturb him, and heaven knows that I have no desire to. I telegraphed Mrs. Clary about mail, and then I went to sleep and I slept until just now.

I never was so near dead in all my life; but you mustn't think for a minute that I'm not having a lovely time, for I am, and it was so kind of Uncle to bring me. Now good-by, and with much love,

Yours,
Yvonne.

The author begs the reader's lenient consideration as to this description of Talbot's Tower. The story was written from notes taken five years ago, since which time the tower has undergone a thorough restoration.

VIII

UNCLE JOHN PARALYZED

"Come in! Come on! Well, don't you hear? Can't you understand any—Oh, it's you, child. I thought it was one of those darned waiters.

"Sit down; pull up a chair by the bed. It's so long since I sent for you that I just about thought that you were not coming. I suppose you were surprised at my sending for you; but it was the only way to do. It's a hard thing to break to you, Yvonne; but you'd have to know in the course of the day, and I always do everything right off that I've not decided to wait and see about. Now don't look frightened, my dear; nobody's *dead*—it's only that I'm paralyzed!

"There, what do you think of that? Yes, it's true for a fact. My legs! I had some premonitory symptoms yesterday going up that cursed old tower, and I had some very advanced ones coming down from it; and this morning, when I started to shave, the truth just burst in my face. Now, don't try to say anything, for I've read too many patent-medicine advertisements not to recognize paralysis when I feel it up and down the back of my own legs. I'm not the man not to know my own feelings, and I want to tell you that when I got up this morning I couldn't stand up, and then, after I stood up, I couldn't sit down; and if that isn't a clear case of having completely given out, I don't know what you would call it.

"Now, my dear, the question is, what's to be done? Of course our travels have come to a full stop, for I shall probably never walk again. The curious thing is that I don't feel any particular inclination ever to walk again. You've no conception of the sentiments that I feel in my legs; but if you roll the fatigue of a lifetime into either the left or the right, you can get some faint inkling of the first freshness of paralysis. I tell you, Yvonne, it is awful. Every cobblestone I've gone over seems to be singing in my calves; but that's neither here nor there. What I want you to do is to go to the pocket of my valise get out the cable-code book and look out a word that means 'Both legs paralyzed. What shall I do with the girls?' You'll find a word that means it, if you look long enough. They've got forty pages of words that mean every fool thing on earth from 'It's a boy' to 'Impossible to lend you ten dollars.' I was reading it over in Paris the other day while I waited for my money at the bank.

"Well, ain't you going to get the code-book? I don't want to be impatient, but I want some one to be doing something. You don't know how restless it makes me to think of lying still for the rest of my life. While I was waiting for you, I was thinking that probably I shall live right here in Caen till I die. I'm very glad we got here too late to see anything, because now I can take it bit by bit and drag it out through my remaining days. I shall have a wheeling-chair and a man to push me around, and—well, maybe it's in the little outside pocket. I know I had it in Paris, anyhow; I remember I was just reading that 'salsify' means 'Your mother-in-law left by the ten o'clock train,' and that 'salsifry' means that she didn't, when they brought me my money, and I was free to go.

"'I'm happy that it will be out of the question for me ever to travel again.'"

"Well, now you've got it. I thought maybe it would be in the little valise all the time. Seems to me the sicknesses begin with 'Salt.' I remember 'Saltfish' means 'have got smallpox; keep away,' and 'Saltpetre' means 'have got a cold; come at once.' You look along there and find 'paralysis.' I'll just keep quiet while you're looking. I'd better be learning to keep quiet. Keeping quiet must be the long suit of the paralyzed, I should fancy. But you see what it is now to be an optimist. Here's my life practically over all of a sudden, and, instead of being blue, I'm as cheerful as a cricket. No need of fussing over the candle-grease on my hat now, for I shall never wear a hat again, I shall wear a soft felt tied over my ears with a plaid shawl as they always do in rolling-chairs; as for the umbrella, I'm actually glad I left it. It would only have been an aggravation to have seen it lying around. But all the same I can't see why you didn't notice it lying down there. It must have been in plain sight,—I remember pointing over at Mont Mirat with it, and saying the rock looked as if it had been dropped there from above.

Yvonne, I tell you when I think of all we did these last two days I feel perfectly content to be paralyzed. I'm glad to think that I've got such a good excuse to stay right in bed; I'm happy that it will be out of the question for me ever to travel again. I feel as if I've traveled enough to last me forever; I actually don't want to see anything more. No more catching trains and climbing castles for your Uncle John—not in his life. You can put the Baedeker in the fire right now—I never want to see a red cover or a green string or an index again as long as I live. What's that? No, I sha'n't want it to look over and recall things by; I can recall more than I want to just by the way I feel. I don't need any guide-book to remember what I've been through since I left Paris. I remember too much. I remember so much that I am rejoiced to think that muscles over which I have no control will prevent my having to go out to-day and see anything else. It seems a little hard to think of having sight-seen so hard that you never want to see another sight, but I'm perfectly content. And I don't want a doctor, either; I've no faith in French doctors. It would be just like one to hypnotize me and set me going again, and I don't want to go. I want to lie right here, and I thank the Lord that I have money enough to allow me to lie here forever, if I feel like it. I was thinking this morning what a horrible existence a tramp must lead—always going on to new places. Thank Heaven, I can just settle down in this old one and stay on indefinitely. I want you to go down to the office and ask what rate they'll make for this room by the year. I want this same room right along. It's the first restful spot I've struck since my trunk went smash into that ship. Yvonne, did you notice the way they handled those trunks when we landed—as if they were eggs? I tell you, the baggage system at home is a burning disgrace. That's one reason I like Europe so—it's quiet and peaceful. I heard some goats go by this morning; I'd like to know a hotel in America where you can listen to a goat. And then that wallpaper, what a tranquil pattern—a basket of sunflowers upside down alternately with a single palm upside up! What a contrast to the paper on that room I sailed from! It looked more like snakes doing physical culture than anything else.

"Yvonne, I was thinking it all over as I lay here this morning waiting for you, and the truth is, we've been traveling too fast. I wanted you to see all there was to see, and I overlooked myself completely. Don't feel badly, child, because I know you never meant it; but it *is* the truth, and, as a consequence, here I lie paralyzed. Yes, we've been traveling too fast. It's the vice of the American abroad; it's the terrible secret drain upon the strength of our better classes. We come over to rest, and if we don't do two countries a week we feel we've wasted our money. The idea of leaving Paris in the morning and doing Chartres and Dreux and getting to Argentan that night! Why, Hercules himself would have been used up. And then that castle at Falaise. But I'm not sorry that I went to Falaise. No, I'm not sorry. Yvonne, there was something about that castle that I'll never get over. I tell you those were the days to live in! I was thinking about it while I was waiting for you this morning. Will you consider what it must have been to put on a suit that you couldn't be punched through, and then get out with an ax that faced two ways and have full freedom to hack at people you hated. I tell you, child, I should have been one of those who barricaded themselves behind the dead bodies they had killed and kept right on firing over the top. And to-day my armor would be hanging up somewhere all full of dents and rusty blood-stains, and I'd be a sight in some cathedral with your Aunt Jane wearing a funnel and an accordion beside me. We'd both be in marble, of course, some worn by time and some chipped by tourists—ah, well!

"Can't you find anything suitable in that code-book? Here, I've been waiting a quarter of an hour for you to hunt—hand me the book. I remember 'Shell' is 'have broken my left leg,' and 'Shellfish' is 'have broken my right leg,' and 'Shawl' is—wait a bit—keep still, Yvonne; no one in the wide world can study a code and listen at the—

"Oh, well, I'll leave it till to-night. Not that I'm irritated at your interruption, for I never let anything ruffle me, and when you write home the first thing I want you to tell your mother is that being paralyzed has not changed me one particle. Same even disposition, same calm outlook on life, same disinclination to ever bother anyone. I want you to make them understand in particular how cheerful I am. Some men would turn cynical at waking up paralyzed, but not me. I feel as if I might get about quite a little in

Caen, maybe even get to Falaise again some time; but you can bank on one thing, and that is that if I ever go back to Falaise I won't go up that tower again. I was wondering this morning as I lay here waiting for you how in thunder you were holding that candle to spill so much grease on my hat. You can't say that you didn't know I was there, for every second step you took your foot hit me in the small of the back. You ought to have gone first, anyhow. I know the rule is for a man to go first going down a staircase, but I don't call that business we were on any staircase; it was more like a series of cascades with us forming the merry, leaping, part. I tell you what, Yvonne, the next time it's up to your Uncle John to play the chamois that springs from crag to crag over an old middle-aged staircase while his niece pours candle-grease on his hat, you can excuse me.

"What I like is clean, open-to-the-day-light ruins like that old one at Jumièges! No peril, no anxiety—all on a level, and time to look up at what wasn't. I tell you, I wouldn't have missed seeing Jumièges for anything. I was thinking this morning as I lay here waiting for you that I have a good mind to write a book about my travels, and that when I do I shall have the frontispiece, me in front of Jumièges. I could take an artist down there on purpose, and while he wasn't doing me, I could look it all over again. Maybe I could go there alone with a kodak and get a satisfactory frontispiece, only those rocks were so thick that most people would think it was a defective plate. I shouldn't like to have them think that, for if I was going to have a book at all, I should have it in good style—gold edges, bevel-plate, and so forth, don't you know. I'd like to write a book about Europe, I vow. I haven't been here very long, but I'll swear I know ten times more than any book ever tells. It never said a word in Baedeker about there not being any cabs at Dreux, or about the condition of those steps in Talbot's Tower, and such things ought to be known. It's all right to make light of perils past, but those steps were too dark for me to ever make light of in this world. Up toward the top where we had to sit down and stretch for the next one—you remember?—I must own that I was honestly sorry I came.

"Well, my child, it must be nearing noon, and I feel like taking a nap before dinner. Suppose you go in and write to your mother and

Mrs. Clary. After your mother gets the cable, she'll naturally be anxious for details, and she won't want to wait longer than ten days to know all. I wish you'd ring and tell them to bring me some hot water before you go; tell them I want it in a pitcher. Make them understand a pitcher. They brought it last night in a sort of brass cylinder, and I couldn't get the thing open anyway—had to use it for a hot-water-bag in bed in the end. It worked fine for that. Never cooled off all night, in fact, I couldn't put my feet against it till morning.

"There, now, you go on and leave me to sleep. You haven't the faintest idea of how used-up I feel. Don't forget to write your mother how cheerful I am; don't forget the hot water. I'll send for you when I want you. There—there—I'm all right, child, don't you worry. Just pull the curtains and let me sleep."

IX

YVONNE TO HER MOTHER

Caen.

Dearest Mama: We are still there, and I'm so happy Uncle is in bed, and at first he thought he was paralyzed, but now he says he's only refusing to take chances. It's so nice having him in bed, because Lee is here, and Uncle makes it all right without knowing anything about it. It was yesterday that he thought he was paralyzed; he sent for me before I was awake to tell me. I was so dreadfully stiff and lame that I thought at first that I could not get up; but of course I did, and went to him as soon as I could. He told me that he was paralyzed, really paralyzed; but I wasn't frightened, because, when he explained his feelings, I knew every one of them, and of course I knew that I wasn't paralyzed. Only when he rolled around upon his pillows and said he certainly would end his days right here in Caen, I couldn't help wishing that he had left me to enjoy my pillows, also.

But he wanted to talk, so I listened for ever so long; and then he wanted to sleep, so I came away to write you, and there was a note from Lee in my room. He was down-stairs waiting, and I went right down, and my, but it was good to see him! I didn't kiss him, because it was a hotel parlor, even if we don't know any one in Caen; but I told him about Uncle, and he said it was fine and that he hoped he would be in bed a week, but no such luck. The yacht has broken a thumb-screw, or whatever it is on a yacht, and they have all come here to meet some automobile people. Lee looks real well; he says he's had no end of fun lately, and that it is a shame I can't go, too.

While we were talking, Mrs. Catherwood-Chigley came in. I didn't know that she was in Europe, and Lee was dreadfully put out for she sat right down and asked all about us. Lee explained that he was here with a yacht and that I was here with Uncle; but she didn't seem to believe us, and shook her head, and asked about Mrs. Clary. She said Mr. Chigley was here, too, and they have seen a monument in the cemetery here that is just what they want for Mr. Catherwood. She says Mr. Catherwood was so clear-cut and Doric in his ideas that it has been very hard to find the right thing. She said Mr. Chigley was out making a sketch of the monument then. She says Mr. Chigley is devotion itself to Mr. Catherwood's memory, and cabled a beautiful wreath on his wedding anniversary and palms tied with purple the day he died. She said she was very happy, and Mr. Chigley just loves to hear her tell stories about Mr. Catherwood by the hour. Lee was awfully rude and kept yawning, and I know she didn't like it by the way she looked at him. It was awfully trying to have her just then, because, of course, there's no telling how long Uncle will stay paralyzed. We really thought she would stay until lunch-time, but Lee yawned so that she went at last.

"Lee was awfully rude and kept yawning, and I know she didn't like it by the way she looked at him."

Lee said that we ought to join them in the touring-cars and do Brittany that way, but he didn't like to tackle Uncle. He says Uncle is a very tough proposition, because he is so devilish observing, and he never begged my pardon for saying it, either. Of course Uncle brought me, and I must do as he wishes, but I do wish that he liked Lee. Lee says he wishes he liked him, too; he says it would be so devilish convenient just now, and he didn't beg my pardon that time, either.

Caen

  I ran up, and Uncle was still asleep, so I had lunch with Lee at the table d'hôte. Mr. Chigley and Mrs. Catherwood-Chigley sat opposite, and she does look so funny with her wedding-rings and engagement-rings alternating on the same finger. Mr. Chigley said he should call on Uncle, and Lee and I were frightened to death until I remembered that Uncle wouldn't be able to read the card or understand the waiter without me. After luncheon I ran up again, and Uncle was still asleep, so we went out to walk. We had a lovely walk, and never looked at a sight, and when we came back I ran up again, and Uncle was still asleep; so Lee and I sat down in the parlor, and we were just going to be so happy when Pinkie and Bunnie Clemens came in. Well, really, I hardly knew either, they have changed so, and Pinkie has a beard and Bunnie is over six feet high. They are on a bicycle tour with eight men, and they saw Elfrida and her sister yesterday, headed for Bayeux. Pinkie says it's been such bad weather they've had to tie umbrellas and waterproofs to them, too. He says Elfrida looks half-witted, and her sister looks like a full idiot. I was so glad that I had on a Paris frock. They wanted me to go to the theater with them, but of course I couldn't, for I couldn't be sure about Uncle's staying paralyzed.

He slept till eight o'clock last night, and then he had dinner and went right to sleep again, so I could have gone to the theater after all; but how could I know to dare to risk it?

Lee and the men from the yacht are at another hotel, so he didn't come very early this morning, and it was fortunate, because Uncle sent for me about nine to explain Mr. Chigley's card, which they poked under the door last night. Uncle was so curious to know what it was that he got out of bed and found he could walk. He said he had never felt sure that it was paralysis, only he wanted to be on the safe side, and he is in bed still, only he is so lively that I am half crazy over Lee. If Uncle concludes he's all right, and comes down and finds Lee, I know he isn't going to like it at all. Pinkie and Bunnie have gone on to Mont St. Michel, and the Catherwood-Chigleys took the train for Dol right after breakfast. Mr. Chigley was very sorry not to see Uncle, and Mrs. Catherwood-Chigley said she should write you all about how well and happy I was looking. I know that what she really means to write about is Lee; but you know all about him, so I don't care.

Lee says if there was time he'd go to Paris and get a nurse and an electric-battery and have Uncle kept just comfortably paralyzed for a few more days, but there isn't time, and I am so worried. If Uncle loses any more patience with Lee, he won't have any patience left at all, and I'll have to go all of the rest of the trip that way. We took a walk this afternoon to consult, and we saw Elfrida and her sister. They have cut off their hair, because it bothered them so, coming down in their eyes, and Elfrida says she feels all the freedom of a man thrilling through her—you know how funny she always talks. They have seven calloused places on the inside of each hand from the handle-bars, and Elfrida says she's sure their insteps will arch forever after. They were coming out of St. Stephen's Church, and the only way to get rid of them was to say that we were just going in; so we said it, and went in.

It was really very interesting, and the tomb of William the Conqueror is there. He built St. Stephen's, and Mathilde built La Trinité at the other end of the town, partly as a thank-offering for conquering England and partly as a penance for being cousins. There was a monastery with St. Stephen's and a convent with La Trinité until the Revolution changed everything. William's tomb is just a flat slab in front of the altar, but he really isn't there any more, for they have dug him up and scattered him over and over again. The church is tremendously big and plain, and every word you even whisper echoes so much that Lee and I thought we'd better come out where we could talk alone.

When we came back to the hotel, I ran up, and the mail had come from Paris; so Uncle said if I'd fill his fountain-pen, he'd just spend the afternoon letting a few people in America know what Europe was really like. I'm a little bit troubled, for I'm all over being stiff and sore from that climbing, and yet he seems to feel almost as mean as ever. He has his meals in his room, for, although we're on the first floor, he says he cannot even think calmly of a stair-case yet. He says that Talbot's Tower seems to have settled in his calves, and Heaven knows when he'll get over it. Lee says I ought not to worry, but to make the most out of the situation; but I do worry, because Uncle is so uncertain. And I'm perfectly positive that there will be an awful scene when he finds out that during his paralysis I've been going all over with Lee.

"He has his meals in his room, for he says he cannot even think calmly of a stair-case yet."

Lee and I went to walk this afternoon, and we visited the old, old church of St. Nicolas. It said in the book that the apse still had its original stone roof, and Lee said it would be a good chance to learn what an apse was; so we set out to go there, but we forgot all about where we set out for, and it was five o'clock before we finally got back to where it was. It stands in an old cemetery, and it says in the book that it has been secularized; so we climbed up on gravestones till we could see in the windows and learn what that meant, also. The gravestones were all covered with lichen and so slippery that in the end Lee gave up and just helped me to look. We didn't learn much, though, for it was only full of hay.

When we got back to the hotel, I ran up, and Uncle was gone! I never was so frightened in my life, and when I ran back and told Lee, he whistled, so I saw that he was upset, too. He said I'd better go to my room and wait, and he'd dine at his hotel to-night; so I went to my room, and Uncle was there, hunting all through my things for the address-book. I was so glad and relieved that I didn't mind a bit the way he had churned everything up, although you ought to see my trunk, and I kissed him and told him it was just splendid to see him beginning to go about again. He looked pleased, but he says the backs of his legs are still beyond the power of description, and so I proposed having dinner with him in his room, which we did very comfortably, and he told me that he should remember this trip till the day he died, without any regard for the grease I spilt on his hat. After dinner he was very fidgety, and I can see that the confinement is wearing on him; but I don't know what to do.

More letters came by the evening mail, and Mrs. Clary is so in raptures over the dinner that when Uncle asked me if I had heard from her I thought it was wisest to say no, because I knew that if he read how happy M. Sibilet was making her, he surely wouldn't like it at all.

Lee sent me a note by a messenger about eleven o'clock, with instructions in French on the outside about their delivering it to me when I was *not* with Uncle. They delivered it all right, and I read it. He just said that the automobiles had come, and that he was going to cast his die clean over the Rubicon to-morrow morning at eleven. That means that he is going, of course, and that I am to be left here all alone. I do feel very badly over it, for Uncle will be almost sure to find out about Lee whenever he can get downstairs again, and then I'm sure I don't know what will happen. Of course I've not done anything that I shouldn't have done; but, dear me! doing right doesn't help if Uncle chooses to decide that it is wrong. And if he can't walk, to let us go on traveling, he's going to keep getting more and more difficult to get along with. I don't like to tell Lee how troubled I am, because if Lee gets worked up and decides to take a hand in while I'm traveling with Uncle, I might as well be Mr. Pickwick when he rushed between just in time to get the tongs on one side and the shovel on the other. I don't want Lee trying to defend me from Uncle, because I know Uncle would never forgive him for thinking I needed defending. You know yourself just how Uncle is, and now that his legs are so stiff he is more that way than ever. Lee doesn't understand, and I can't make him understand, and perhaps it's just as well that he should go on to-morrow. Maybe Uncle will be better in a few days, so that we can visit Bayeux. He's crazy to go to Bayeux and see the tapestry, and it isn't so very far. But what shall we do if we come to any town again where there are no cabs! It would be awful.

However, I shall not worry, for it's no use. Mrs. Catherwood-Chigley wrote me her address on one of her cards, and Lee took it and sent it to me with some beautiful flowers. He thought it was such a clever, safe idea; but just suppose we meet them again! If I didn't think Lee was just right, I'd think he had almost too many clever ideas; and, anyhow, I know that I'm sure that he has too many while I'm traveling with Uncle.

Now, good-night, it's so very late. Don't ever feel troubled over me, for I'm having a splendid time, and it was so kind of Uncle to bring us.

Your own loving
Yvonne.

X

YVONNE TO HER MOTHER

Vire.

Dear Mama: I am the happiest thing in the whole wide world, and Lee is the grandest fellow! I must write you everything, and you will see.

The morning after I last wrote, Uncle had me waked up at seven and wrote on a scrap of paper, "We leave for Bayeux at 8.30." I was just about sick, for I knew he wasn't able to, and then, besides, if we left so early, I surely shouldn't see Lee again. But I got up and dressed, of course, and I was beside myself to find some way of sending Lee a scrap of a good-by before we took a cab for the *gare*. Uncle was in high spirits over getting out again, and all went well until it came the minute to get him on to the train. Well, I do believe he was scared himself. Getting on to a French train is almost like going up a ladder that slopes the wrong way, I always think, and it took two commissionaires to hoist Uncle into the coupé. He was awfully worried over it, I could see, for he talked about what an outrageous idiot Mr. Chopstone was all the way to

Bayeux. We had to get out there, of course, and I was beside myself to know how to manage. In the end Uncle came down so suddenly that he nearly crushed me and a meek, good-hearted little Frenchman who had kindly offered to help assist.

Bayeux

The *gare* at Bayeux is quite a walk from the part of the town where the sights are and there wasn't a cab or a thing on wheels. I didn't dare look at Uncle, for there is no train back till four in the afternoon. He seemed a bit staggered at first, and then he said well, it was level, and we'd go leisurely along and enjoy the fresh, pure, sweet air of the country. So we walked along, but I could see he wasn't enjoying it a bit, and it took us a half-hour to get to where we were going. We went to the cathedral first, and Uncle sat right down and said he wanted time enough to enjoy the ground-work of the vaulting and that I could just leave him and go around alone. It was my first chance to look at anything as slow as I liked, and I really did enjoy myself very much.

It's a really wonderful old cathedral, and I found a nice old sacristan behind the altar, and he took me underneath into the crypt, and the crypt is the original church where Harold took the oath. It was slowly buried by the dirt of centuries, and when they started to put a furnace in a few years ago, they found it and dug it out again. It isn't very large, and the walls are of stone several feet thick, with little bits of arched windows set up too high to see from.

When I came back we went to see the tapestry in the museum, and it isn't really tapestry at all: it's a long, long strip of linen about a foot wide, with scenes embroidered on it in Kensington, and over and over. It's really very well done, and it isn't a bit badly worn out—only a few little holes here and there. The scenes are very interesting, and some of them are awfully funny. The way they hauled the horses over the sides of the boats when they landed in England, for example. The Saxons have beards, and the Normans are shaven. I couldn't help thinking how funny it was that the Normans, who were regarded as barbarians by the French, were looked upon as tremendously effete by the English. Uncle took a deal of pleasure studying the whole thing, and we were there till it was time for lunch. We had a nice lunch at a clean little place, and then came the rub. There was nothing to do till train-time, and that terrible walk to the *gare*. I had brought a book along, so I could read aloud, but Uncle said only a woman would come to Bayeux and read a novel, and that I reminded him of Aunt Jane. You know how terrible it is when any one reminds him of Aunt Jane; so I closed the book at once, and said I'd do anything he liked. He said that that was more like Aunt Jane than ever, to just sit back and throw the whole burden on to him; and then he shook his watch and held it to his ear and said "Hum!" too, one right after the other. I was almost beside myself to know what to do or what to suggest, and just then something came puffing up behind us and stopped right at our side. It was a big automobile, with three men in it, and one jerked off his mask and jumped out over the wheel and grabbed Uncle by the hand. And it was Lee!

"And it was Lee"

You never saw anything like Uncle's face! He seemed reparalyzed for a few seconds, and Lee kept shaking his hand and telling him how glad he was to see him, and how he *must* get right into the automobile and go on with them to Caen. My heart just about stopped beating, I was so anxious, but Lee never stopped shaking, and the other men took off their masks and got out, too, and told Uncle he really must do them the honor and give them the pleasure, and in the end we got him in, and Lee won out.

Oh, it was such fun! We had the most glorious trip back to Caen. They had an extra mask along, and Uncle wore it and sat on the front seat, and Mr. Peters, the man who owns the automobile, was really lovely to him. The other man and Lee and I sat behind, and the other man is Mr. Peters's mother's son by her second husband. His name is Archie Stowell, and I should judge that Mr. Peters's mother's second husband was a lot livelier than the first, but not so clever. Mr. Peters is really awfully clever, and the way he talked to

Uncle was wonderful. Uncle said it was a very smooth-riding automobile, and Mr. Peters said it did him good all through to meet some one who recognized the good points of a good machine at once; he said not one man in a thousand had brains enough to know a good machine when he was in it, and that he was overjoyed to have accidentally met the one man who did discriminate. And Uncle said he should judge that automobiling was a very easy way of getting over the ground when one was traveling in Europe, and Mr. Peters said it was perfectly bewildering how the breadth and scope of Uncle's mind could instantaneously seize and weigh every side of an intricate proposition and as instantaneously solve it completely. By the time we reached Caen Uncle was so saturated with Mr. Peters that he even smiled on Lee as we got out and asked them all three to dine with us at eight. They accepted, and went to their hotel to dress, and Uncle went to his room without one word of any kind to me.

They came, and we had a very nice dinner in a little separate room, and the way Mr. Peters talked to Uncle was worth listening to surely. And when Uncle was talking, he leaned forward and paid attention as if his life depended on every word. By ten o'clock Uncle was happier than I have almost ever seen him, and Mr. Peters said it was no use, we just simply must join their party and go on in the automobile. Lee began to laugh when he said that, and said: "Now, Peters, you'll learn the sensation of getting turned down cold." It was an awful second for me, because I just felt Uncle's terrible battle between not wanting to go on with Lee and wanting to contradict him; but in the end the wanting to contradict overpowered everything else, and he said: "Young man, when you are as old as I am you'll be less ready to speak for other people than you seem disposed to do now."

"We passed Elfrida and her sister to-day, pedaling along for dear life"

And then he accepted Mr. Peters's invitation! So will you only please to think of it—we are touring with Lee, and to-day we came up through the lovely valley of the Vire to this little town of the same name. It is all too nice for words; Uncle sits on the front seat all the time, and when he gives Mr. Peters advice, Mr. Peters always thanks him and says that he never met any one before with sense enough to have figured that out.

We passed Elfrida and her sister to-day, pedaling along for dear life. They didn't know us, and they are getting to look so awful that I thought it was just as well. Uncle says he thinks they are seeing Europe for thirty cents a day now.

It is raining, and I must go to bed.

Your very happy,
Yvonne.

XI

YVONNE TO HER MOTHER

Vire.

Dearest Mama: We are still here in Vire, and we cannot go on for it is raining awfully. It rained all yesterday, and we had *more* fun. About ten in the morning an automobile arrived with a lady Lee knows named Mrs. Brewer and three men, and about twelve another automobile arrived with Clara and Emily Kingsley and their aunt Clara Emily and Ellsworth Grimm and Jim Freeman and a chauffeur, and about half-past one a runabout automobile camein with the two Tripps. We are like a big house-party, and Mr. Peters plays poker with Uncle every minute, so we. can all have no end of a good time

I must explain to you about Mr. Peters, because Lee explained to me. I was so troubled over Mr. Peters being so devoted to Uncle and never winning a single jack-pot once himself that Lee told me all about how it is. It seems that Mr. Peters's mother was married to Mr. Peters's father for quite a while before he died and that Mr. Peters's father wasn't very well off and was very hard to live pleasantly with on account of Mr. Stowell's father, who lived next door and was very well off and very easy for Mr. Peters's mother to get along with always; Mr. Peters's father died when Mr. Peters was about twelve years old, and just as soon as it was perfectly ladylike, Mr. Peters's mother married Mr. Stowell's father and went next door to live and had Mr. Stowell. Lee says Mr. Stowell's father never liked Mr. Peters much because he reminded him of all those years that Mr. Peters's and Mr. Stowell's mother lived next door instead of living with him; but Lee says Mr. Peters is very clever, and he saw how much his father lost from not being easy to get along with, and so he made up his mind to be easy to get along with himself. He gets along so well with Mr. Stowell that they travel together all the time, and Lee says he told him that if he could get along well with Uncle he'd make it well worth his while; so he's getting along beautifully with Uncle, and Lee is making it ever so well worth his while.

Clara Kingsley has fallen in love with one of the men who came with Mrs. Brewer—the tall, dark one, who does not talk much and reads German in his room most of his time. There are so many that I get names mixed, but Emily Kingsley is the same as ever, and *such* a joy to meet again. She says she doesn't fall in love the way

Clara does; she only gets badly spattered. The two Tripps are both devoted to Emily, and I think they are all sort of keeping along together. Miss Clara Emily asked after every one in our family, even Aunt Jane. Of course I told her that Aunt Jane had been dead two years, and you ought to have seen her jump and look at Uncle. She asked me if Uncle lived alone in the house, and she looked so reflective that I felt quite uncomfortable. I told Lee about it, but he says Uncle must take his chances the same as the rest of the world when it comes to Miss Clara Emily. I wish Lee wouldn't make light of anything so serious as the way Miss Clara Emily looked reflective. You know you wouldn't like her having all Aunt Jane's lace, and I'm sure that after Uncle was completely married to her, he wouldn't like it at all, either. I don't know what Mrs. Brewer is, but the men that came in the automobile with her are just devoted to her, and she makes every one have a good time. We played cards and Consequences all the afternoon, and Mrs. Brewer told our fortunes from tea-leaves in the evening. She told Uncle to beware of a long, pointed nose which she saw in his cup, and Miss Clara Emily didn't know whether to be mad or glad. She saw a wedding-ring in Lee's cup, and I blushed terribly and tried to cough, and sneezed instead; and Lee said it was an automobile tire, and meant a breakdown. I do think Lee is always so nice. But about eleven we all got a terrible shock, for the handsome man that Clara has fallen in love with suddenly came to the door with his German book in his hand and said to Mrs. Brewer, "Come to bed, Bert. I'm sleepy as the devil."

   You never saw anything like poor Clara! I thought that she would faint, for you know when Clara falls in love how it goes all through her. She went upstairs a little later, and, as luck would have it, she had the next room to the Brewers, and she says it just about killed her to hear him brushing his teeth, and I promised her I'd never tell, but she says he called her and Emily the "Yellow Kids" and laughed and laughed and laughed. I do think it was very horrid of him, for they can't help having Mr. Kingsley's ears, and I comforted Clara all I could, and told her that the way she puffs her hair is ever so becoming. It isn't a bit, but I had to be as nice as I knew how, for she was crying so that I was afraid Mr. Brewer would call her *Cyrano de Bergerac*, if she didn't stop.

I had the room between Uncle and the two Tripps, and the two Tripps calculated their money for three solid hours, I do believe, trying to see whether they'd have to draw on Paris behind them or could wait for London ahead. The big Tripp said Mr. Peters had a hard row to hoe and the little Tripp said Lee had a soft snap, and then they added and subtracted and divided for another hour. I was almost insane when finally the little Tripp said: "Tell me what fifteen times nine is, and then I'll go to sleep," and someone across the hall hollered: "In Heaven's name tell him what fifteen times nine is, and then we'll *all* go to sleep." There was deadly stillness after that.

(NEXT DAY)
Vire.
Dearest Mama:

You see, we are still here and it is still raining. Every one telegraphed for mail yesterday and every one got it to-day. I had your letters and one from Edna and one from Mrs. Clary. They are going on a coaching trip with the man who wasn't a duke, and Edna has bought three new hats. Mrs. Clary says I am an angel and that she and Edna think it right out of Heaven the way Lee has turned up. I had three letters from Mr. Edgar, and he says he is thinking of making a trip into Brittany and joining us. I told Lee, and Lee says he isn't thinking anything of the kind, not in his life. I don't really think that Mr. Edgar and Lee would get on very well together. I feel almost sure that they wouldn't like each other. Indeed, I feel quite sure.

Poor Clara came to my room while I was reading letters, and she says she is blighted by Mr. Brewer and knows she can never get over it. She says she wouldn't have him know that she has the next room and can hear every word for anything, for she says it's perfectly awful all she's overhearing. She says he called Mrs. Brewer "Ladybug," and it sounded so sweet that she cried for fifteen minutes with the pillow around her head to keep them from hearing her. I'm awfully sorry about Clara, because she is always so sincere. Don't you remember that time that she was so sincere that they were afraid that she would commit suicide over Cleever Wiggins—and that awfully sincere time she had with young Prof.

Cook? She says she could stand anything if she could feel that she was reciprocated; but she says she can't feel that Mr. Brewer reciprocates one bit, for he told his wife that he bet Clara would be an older maid than her aunt before she got through with life, and Clara says that's no compliment, however you work it.

  When we went down-stairs, Mr. Peters and Uncle were playing poker and Miss Clara Emily was sitting by them looking rapt. Heavens! I do hope it will stop raining and let us get away soon, for Uncle told me this noon that she was more unlike Aunt Jane than any woman that he had seen in years. Lee says he hopes we can get away very soon, too; he does not like Ellsworth Grimm. It is a pity, because Ellsworth has grown so nice, and with his pointed beard he is really very handsome. He has done a beautiful sketch of me that every one but Lee thinks is splendid, and I'm going to send it to you when it is finished. Uncle is very good-tempered, and has won over a hundred and fifty francs from Mr. Peters at poker. Mr. Peters says he's played poker for years without meeting such a rattling winner as Uncle, and Uncle believes him. The two Tripps want to go on, too, because they decided to wait for their money at London, and they are afraid they are going to run short. Mr. Brewer wants to go, too, because he has finished his German book. I think we all want to go, because two days is a long while to spend in Vire. Clara says if they cannot go on in the automobile, she must take a train, for she is getting more and more sincere the more she is hearing Mr. Brewer talking to his wife through the wall. Clara says he said that he was going to snip her nose off when they were dressing this morning, and she says he calls her "Puss" till Clara feels as if she should expire in agony. She doesn't get any sympathy from Emily, because Emily has another room, and Emily isn't sincere, anyhow. Emily has thrown over the two Tripps and taken Mr. Stowell, and thrown over Mr. Stowell and gone back to the big Tripp, all in just these two days. Emily asked me if I ever saw such a fool as Clara; she says it almost kills her to have such a sister and such an aunt. She asked me if I'd noticed her aunt looking at my Uncle, and I had to say yes. Then she said she did hope that it would stop raining pretty soon, for she wants to get to Granville and meet a man and get letters from three more.

"Miss Clara Emily is getting very much in earnest"

Uncle came into my room this afternoon noon and said the more he saw of Europe the better he liked it, and that Mr. Peters was the sort of friend that was worth making. He said he had decided to go on with them to Mont St. Michel, because they were so urgent that he couldn't well get out of it. He says he hopes I won't consider that he has changed his opinion of Lee because he hasn't, but that he will say this much, and that is, that the fact that a man like Mr. Peters will call Lee his friend proves that he must have some good in him somewhere. Uncle said the Kingsleys seem to be nice girls, and then he coughed, but I didn't say anything, so he dropped the subject. I must tell you, though, that Miss Clara Emily is getting very much in earnest, and every one is noticing it, and Uncle seems pleased.

We all played cards to-day and wrote letters and Lee told Ellsworth Grimm he was a blank idiot under his breath. I don't know what was the trouble, and Lee says it isn't any of my business, but I think we are all getting cross from being shut up so much in this little country hotel. Elfrida and her sister arrived about noon, but there wasn't any spare room under two francs, and so they went to the other hotel. Ellsworth Grimm has gone to the other hotel, too. He says it rains in his ceiling and he's afraid he'll get pneumonia.

It's getting awful about poor Clara and Mr. Brewer, for he said something about her to-day that almost killed her, and that is so bad that she won't repeat it to me. She says Mrs. Brewer just shrieked with laughter over it, and told him he was the dearest, horridest thing alive. Clara says I cannot possibly guess the torture of being sincere over a married man who howls with laughter over you in the next room. She says she can't help hearing, and she's taken an awful cold standing with her ear to the wall, too. Poor Clara!

Emily and the big Tripp went out and walked in the rain most all the afternoon, and I thought she must be very fond of him to be willing to get so wet; but she says all she's done here she's done to make Jim Freeman jealous. I was so surprised when she told me that, for Jim has spent the entire two days with the chauffeur under the automobile. They have only come out to eat and sleep, and if he is in love with Emily, he is certainly taking it easy.

Vire (12 M. next day).

Oh, Mama, we are so tired of this place! Clara has cried herself sick, and her aunt sent for the doctor. Mr. and Mrs. Brewer heard through the wall when he came, and heard that it was Clara, and of course they knew that Clara must have heard them just as well as they could hear the doctor, and they nearly went crazy. Mrs. Brewer came to me in a sort of mad despair and said Mr. Brewer was almost wild. She says she has mimicked Clara and Emily and their aunt over and over, and she never dreamed that the wall was so thin. She says Mr. Brewer talks all the time he dresses and undresses and says anything that comes into his head. They felt perfectly unable to face Clara again, and it was raining so hard that they couldn't go on, so they moved over to the other hotel.

Vire (2 p.m. same day).

It's very funny, but it seems that the little Tripp was dreadfully taken with Mrs. Brewer, so the two Tripps have moved over to the other hotel, too. Mr. Stowell and Emily want to go, too, but they are with parties, and cannot do as they please. The big Tripp came back for his soap, and said he had a fireplace and now Uncle wants to move, too.

Vire (4 p.m. same day).

We did move, and Lee said if we went, he was going. So he and Mr. Peters and Mr. Stowell have come over. So we are all here except the Kingsleys and Jim Freeman. I had to go back for Uncle's soap, and the little Tripp left his pajamas, so we went back together to get both, and poor Clara is delirious, screaming, "Yellow kids, yellow kids!" every minute. Every one thinks she is thinking of shopping in Paris, and I didn't explain; but while we were there, Mr. Brewer came back for their soap and heard Clara, and, as a result, he and his wife went on in their automobile, rain or no rain. They left one of their men named Scott McCarthy, and took Ellsworth Grimm. Ellsworth wanted to go, and Scott wanted to stay, so it happened very nicely.

Vire (6 p.m. same day).

They have just moved Clara over here. She had a fresh fit when she heard Mr. Brewer getting the soap, and Miss Clara Emily thought that a change of scene would benefit her; so they all moved over. Emily told me (I walked over with Emily when she went back to get their soap) that it really wasn't Clara at all: it was that her aunt wanted to keep close to my Uncle. Isn't it awful? And Uncle is so flattered, too! I do hope that it will stop raining tomorrow. Lee doesn't like Scott McCarthy, and it is a pity, for he seems to be such a nice man. It's terribly dull without Mrs. Brewer, she was so lively. Mr. Peters is beginning to look real pale, and Lee says he ought to have a monument to patience erected to him. Jim Freeman is worried over the automobiles; he's afraid something will happen to them on account of our all changing hotels. Wouldn't that be terrible?

Lovingly,
Yvonne.

Vire (8 a.m. next day).

p.s. Just a line to say that the sun has come out, and that we are all going on by train, except Jim Freeman and the chauffeur. Some one slashed all the automobile tires last night. Isn't that awful?

XII

UNCLE JOHN AND MONT-SAINT-MICHEL

"Well, this is a great change from the automobile—eh, Peters? Of all the outrageous, heathenish actions, that cutting of automobile tires was the worst. Every man at that hotel ought to be hung up and high-strung and quartered—make an example of the whole outfit. I must say, though, that I blame Freeman a good deal myself. He says he felt anxious, and yet he never had that chauffeur set up to watch. Foolish, very foolish; but he'll pay the penalty, having to stay there and wait for the tires from Caen.

"Lee, if you could withdraw yourself somewhat from the window, perhaps I could form some faint conception of what the country looks like to the north. If you and Yvonne want to compare maps, I should suggest that you sit side by side instead of holding the map so that it completely covers my horizon.

"Well, Peters, and so here we are off for Dol. Dol seems to be the only way to get in or out of Brittany and it must have been so always, for in Matilda's tapestry she's got William and Harold on their way to Dol as a beginning to making things hot for the Lord of Brittany. Very interesting study, that tapestry, Peters. I wouldn't have—

"Stowell, I beg your pardon, but those are my feet, and not valises, that you are going to sleep against. I didn't say anything as long as you took them as they lay, but now that you want my left foot slanting to the right, I must protest. Suppose you end yourself the other way for a change, anyhow.

"Well, Peters, and so we are off for Mont-Saint-Michel, bless her old heart—or is Michel a him? I must say, I'm deeply interested in to-day's expedition. Wasn't some English Henry shut up on Mont-Saint-Michel and fed by ravens there, or something like that? Yes;

I know there's some such legend, and now we're going to see the spot. How do we get from Dol to the mont? By Pontorson, eh? And then diligence the rest. Well, I must say it sounds like quite an undertaking; but then, if you leave the beaten path, you must always pay the price, and I must say I enjoy these little jaunts with a congenial party. Too bad the Kingsleys couldn't have continued with us. Nice people, the Kingsleys—very interesting girls. What did you say? Oh, yes, of course the aunt was interesting, too; but—what did you say? Nonsense, nonsense! But I will say one thing, Peters, and that is that it pays to travel around when it brings one in contact with people such as yourself and Miss Kingsley.

"So this is Pontorson! Do we get down here? Is that the diligence? Do we get up there? Great Scott! how can we? And it looks to be about full already. Do you mean that we have got to climb that little ladder? I don't believe Yvonne can. I don't believe she ought to, even if she can. Can't we go to Mont-Saint-Michel some other way? Peters, I'd like to slay with my own hands that wretch that slashed our automobile. Will you think of the difference he is making in our comfort these days?

"Well, Stowell, let's see you skin up there first. Looks easy, don't it, Peters? Lee, you go next. Now, Peters, it's your turn. And now, Yvonne, my child, steady, and start and keep right on to the end. There—there—catch her on top anywhere, Peters. Got her? Are you all right, child? And now for your Uncle John!

"Ask him if this is a new ladder. I don't want to take any chances with an old ladder, you know. Well, what did he say? Ask him if people ever do fall or meet with any sort of accidents going up. Well, what did he say? Peters, this looks more serious every minute. What do they have the thing so high for, anyhow? I must say I don't like going up there at all. Ask him if he has ever known anyone to miss their footing? Well, tell him to keep a good grip on the ladder. Now then, one, two,—oh, this is—confound him! tell him to steady it—Great Scott! Landed!

"And now that I am up, tell me how in all creation I'm ever to get down again.

"Well, why don't we start? That's the worst of Europe, Peters—no push, no energy. Perfectly content to sit on a diligence and stagnate. Let me look at my watch. Eleven. Well, I'm not at all surprised. I wouldn't be surprised at anything that might occur in this vicinity. I tell you, Peters, it will be a glad day for me when I set my foot down hard on a New York steamer pier once more. I can't but feel—

"Ah, so we are to get under way at last! Lumbering old concern—eh, Peters? Great contrast to the automobile—Lee, as there may be some one speaking English within a mile of us, I would suggest that you lower your voice a trifle and give the other fellow a chance. What? I don't catch what you say? Speaking to *me*? Who's speaking to me? *You?* Well, what do you want to say to me? I'm right here to be spoken to, and from the outlook I should fancy that I was going to be right here for an indefinite length of time. Well, what is it? The Brewers! Where? Ahead there? How do you know? Are you sure? What do you think, Peters? Yes, that's them. Brewer seems to be underneath the machine. Well, what shall we do? Wave and holler? We can't do anything else if we want to. But they are going to be a good deal surprised to see us perched aloft like this. Yes; there's Mrs. Brewer sitting on the bank with McCarthy and the other man. I'd rather be the guests than the owner when it comes to an automobile any day.

"Well, why don't you holler, Lee? That's it—make a trumpet out of your hands and just give it to them. Gee! but they are surprised! Holler that we are going to Mme. Poulard Aîné. I suppose that they're going there, too, anyway; no one ever goes anywhere else. Dear me! but they're happy to have that automobile. Lucky for them that they went on just when they did. There's Brewer crawling out from under. Well, I can't stay twisted any longer, so we'll turn our eyes once more to the future.

"What's that ant-hill out at sea? It isn't the sea, though, is it? It's land; gray sand, I vow. And so that is Mont-Saint-Michel? Curious. Used to be on land, eh, and then got to be on sea? It appears to me that we have quite a drive before us yet. Looks to me to be three or four miles. What do you say, Peters? Of course I don't know, how big the mont is, so I have nothing to judge the distance by; but I should say three miles at least.

"Stowell, I've heard that story you are telling ever since I was born; who ever told you that it was new ought to be shot. This tendency to tell old stories is a perfect vice with some people,

Peters, and that brother of yours is forever doing it. I've heard him tell about calling the cabman a pig in France and asking him if he was engaged in Germany until I'm about to the end of my patience. Great Scott! how hot the sun is, and no matter how gaily we lumber along, the mont looks to be equally distant. What is this road we're on, anyway? Seems to be a highway in the most literal sense of the word. Dike, eh? Built on purpose for tourists, I suppose—the American tourists before all, I'll bet.

"Well, so that is the mont close to. Appears to just comfortably cover up the whole island. Curious collection of houses and staircases topped off by a church. However, my main care at this moment isn't what we've come to see, but how in thunder we're to get down to see it. Well, the people line up pretty thick, and they have the additional joy of knowing that every last one of us is a tourist. That's one good thing about America, Peters, you can travel there without being a tourist. You pay a stiff price for very little, but that little's good, and the game ends with it. Europe's entirely different: what turns on the light over the wash-stand turns it off over the bed, and then, with all that, they mark light extra in the bill. There don't seem to be any legitimate hotel comforts here: they're all extra. I vow, I hate to take that hard-wood bolster out from under my head nights, for it's the one thing I get for nothing in every hotel.

"Well, Yvonne, I think you'd better go down first. You go next, Stowell, and then you, Lee. You and I, Peters, will wait and take our time. I vow, I'm not very keen on this descent. Just hold my hat, will you? Here, you, down there, hold this ladder steady. Peters, I—where's the next step? Peters, you—where's the bottom? I vow I—

"Safe at last! quaint old place—old wall with a gate in it, eh! Fishing-rods and oars all about; when does the tide come in? Faster than a horse can gallop, eh? Well, that must be sad for the horse. Anyhow, I didn't ask how fast it came in; I asked when it would come in next. Well, ask some one. An hour after we leave, eh? Interesting. But come on; let's go up to Mme. Poulard Aîné and eat the omelet, and then we can climb around some. You walk on, Yvonne, and order the luncheon, and Mr. Peters and I will come leisurely after. Yes, my niece is a pretty girl, Peters, but nothing but a child—nothing but a child. No more idea of worldliness than a cat has of a cactus; a great responsibility to travel with—a great responsibility. Between you and me, I used to suspect young Reynolds of paying her attention; but when he took another ship over, and then left Paris before we arrived, I saw my suspicions had been wrong. I said a thing or two about him to Yvonne, and she took it perfectly placidly, so then I saw that it was all off. I don't like to run down a friend of yours, Peters,—and I suppose he must be a friend of yours or you wouldn't have him along with you,—but you're old enough to see that he hasn't got the stuff in him to make any girl happy. He's too—too—well, I can't just express it, but I know that you understand. It takes peculiar attributes to make a woman happy. Now, take me for example. My wife and I were very happy; she always knew just what was expected of her, and she always did it. It followed naturally that—

"And so this is the famous omelet-place. Well, in we go. Quaint—very quaint. Look at the chickens turning on the spit and dripping in a trough. My, but they look good! Mme. Poulard herself, isn't it? Good day, ma'am; bon jour—bon jour. Glory, what a smile, stereoscoped and illuminated! Makes me think of the china cat's head that we used to put a candle inside of when I was a kid. Do we go upstairs? Eat up there, eh? Quaint—very quaint. Every fellow did what he pleased to these walls, evidently. Well, Peters, let's sit down."

"And so we now set out to climb Mont-Saint-Michel. Picturesque flight of steps. No, I don't mind climbing—good exercise. Curious little winding walk; old woman with baskets to sell. No, we don't want any; go 'way, go 'way. Terrible nuisance such people. Here's another with yellow flowers. No, no, go 'way, you—and another with matches. No, no, go 'way. Well, that's a pretty tall flight of steps, isn't it, Peters? But I guess we can make it. Where's Yvonne? Ahead, eh? Well, I presume those two fellows can look out for her. Curious about the Brewers not turning up; suppose he's under the automobile yet? Wonder how Freeman is getting on in Vire. Let's stop and look at the view. Fine view! As I was saying, Peters, it was too bad the way we broke up at Vire. I really felt mean over leaving as we did. What did you say? Nonsense; none of that, Peters, none of that. But I will say one thing for her: she certainly was a woman of great perception—always thoughtful for others. Did you notice how she used to push the ash-receiver toward me? It's things like that that make a man comfortable. Astonishing that such a woman should never marry. Well, let's go on. Not more than ninety more steps and two flower women to get over. Peters, have you observed how many stairs there are in Europe? It fairly bristles with them. We go pretty nearly stair-free with us, and over here it's stairs from dawn till—

"Great Scott, will you look at them! Oh, I never can go up there, never! We may as well go back. If you want to, you can go up; but I couldn't possibly see anything that would compensate me for those steps. I'll bet there are ten thousand, and like as not there are more beyond. I'm going back and sit with Mme. Poulard Aîné till it's time to go. You go on alone. Just tell him we don't want any of those oyster-shell pincushions first, will you? Then you go on by yourself, Peters, I've had enough."

XIII

YVONNE TO HER MOTHER

St. Malo.

Dearest Mama: We are all here together again except the Brewers and the two Tripps and Ellsworth Grimm. It is very jolly, only I am so worried over Uncle and Miss Clara Emily. Even Mr. Peters cannot keep them apart. Lee took Mr. Peters to his room and talked to him seriously, and offered to make Uncle still more worth his while; but Mr. Peters has been agreeable so long that he doesn't do it well any more. He just looks silly, and Lee says if he was us he'd let Uncle go rip. But of course Lee isn't us, and I know that he can't be expected to know just how we feel. If Uncle John marries Miss Clara Emily, I know no one is going to like it at all.

In Mont-Saint-Michel

We went to Mont-Saint-Michel, and every one but Uncle went up, and he went seven flights up—he *says* twenty, but I don't believe that there are more than sixteen or seventeen in all. We were ahead, and never knew that he had stopped being behind, and it was so interesting on top that I forgot I had an uncle. There are beautiful halls and cloisters, and then one goes down through all sorts of horrors while the guide tells who lived five years in this hole and who lived twelve years under those steps. You get to have such a contempt for people who were in prison only one or two years over here—as if they ought to be ashamed of only having been in such a short time. There is a ghostly, ghastly museum in Mont-Saint-Michel where the visitors walk through an unlighted gallery and look in at wax victims doing different things in a very thoughtful manner—all but one man who walked on the sand and was overtaken by the tide, and *he* looks anything but thoughtful. The best was the battle, which was very realistic and must have been very trying to the leaders; for how could they get absorbed in a fight when the tide would drown them if they kept on a minute too long? There was a man who thought he would escape, and dug a way out with his nails, taking a short life-time to the task; and then he found he'd dug in instead of out, and, after letting himself down with a rope, he came to a bottom all covered with skeletons. I can assure you that I was glad we were all together and that Lee had my arm tight, for the scenes were awful, and I grew so sick toward the last that when we came down at the end and found Uncle sitting on the ramparts with Miss Clara Emily, I nearly screamed. They had all come while we were above, and Emily and some men were out walking on the sand. Clara is somewhat better; but I think she is even more sincere than usual this time. In her locket she has some plaster from the wall that she heard through, and she says she sleeps with it pressed to her lips. And I *know* that Miss Clara Emily is going to do everything in the world to get Uncle, for Emily says she was traveling just with a little hand-satchel, and now she insists on a suit-case. Oh, dear, I don't know what to do; and Lee is tired of the situation, and wants to go yachting, and I want to go with him. It would be so lovely off yachting with Lee; and the yacht is anchored where we can see her from the city walls. Lee is forever pointing to her. He says Mr. Stowell would let him have her for a month, any day.

We passed the Brewers on our way to Mont-Saint-Michel, but they must have seen the Kingsleys and gone back. Mrs. Brewer told me in Vire that they could never meet the Kingsleys again; she said that Mr. Brewer said if he should meet Clara he knew he should explode. I don't think that Mr. Brewer has much heart or he never would have called poor Clara a Yellow Kid; I've known Clara ever since I was a baby, and it never struck me that she looked like that till she told me that Mr. Brewer said so.

We all took the tram-ride to Rocabey yesterday, but one is so afraid that a wave will wash over the car and drench every one with spray that it isn't much fun. The tide is so funny all along this coast, because the coast is so level that a foot of water covers a mile or so, and when a wave starts to come in there's nothing to stop it at all. I don't think that St. Malo is very interesting, but perhaps that is just Uncle and Miss Clara Emily. He sends her violets, and I know it is he, for it couldn't be Mr. Peters or Mr.

Stowell, and it wouldn't be Jim Freeman or Scott McCarthy. She wears them pinned on in such a funny way.

"Uncle sitting on the ramparts with Miss Clara Emily"

(NEXT DAY)
St. Malo.

Dearest Mama: Edna has sent me the letter about your coming over, and I am so relieved. Perhaps you will get here in time to save Uncle from Miss Clara Emily; I do hope so. Edna's things must be lovely, and I read her letter to Lee. He says if I'm good I will have some things of my own some day, and I do hope so; but Uncle is so heavy on my mind that I cannot realize that I shall ever have any life except trying to keep him from Miss Clara Emily. Mr. Peters is no good at all any more, and has a bad cold besides. He and Clara sit on the ramparts and gaze at the sea, and look as if they were two consolation prizes that the people who won didn't care enough about to take home with them. Lee says he never realized that Mr. Peters could peter out quite so completely. Lee wants to go yachting, and wants me to go, too, and I can't leave Uncle, and Uncle won't leave Miss Clara Emily. It's quite stupid here at St. Malo, and we want to go on; but Lee won't go on, and I'd rather stay in a stupid place with Lee than go anywhere without him. He's mad over the Kingsleys tagging along, because he likes Scott McCarthy less and less all the time. Scott walks on the other side of me sometimes, and Lee doesn't like it. I think land is getting on Lee's nerves, and he ought to go yachting; but life is such a tangle just now that I don't know what to do about anything. Miss Clara Emily is hemstitching a handkerchief, and I just know that it is for Uncle. Oh, dear.

(NEXT DAY)
St. Malo.
Dearest Mama: Such an awful thing almost happened! Clara had a nightmare, and came near choking to death on Mr. Brewer's plaster—the locket, you know. Uncle says only a prompt, efficient, quick-witted, thoroughly capable nature like Miss Clara Emily's could have saved her. Oh, I just know he's becoming serious, and Lee says it's just tommy-rot about the efficiency, because all in the world that Miss Clara Emily did was to jerk the locket up by the chain; and she did that in such an awfully quick way that poor Clara says she's cured of Mr. Brewer forever. She will have to eat soup through a china straw for several days.

Uncle wants to go to Carnac and see the ruins of the Stone Age, and he and Miss Clara Emily are mapping out a trip. I'm sure I don't know what I'll do, for Scott McCarthy has bet Mr. Stowell ten dollars that Uncle gets "hooked" in Carnac. Lee told me, and Lee himself is provisioning the yacht, and says he's cock-sure that he eats some of those provisions aboard of her himself. Emily doesn't want to go to Carnac, and Jim Freeman says it isn't any automobile country, on account of the relics of the Stone Age being so thick in the roads.

(NEXT DAY)

St. Malo.

Dearest Mama: Why didn't you write me that Mrs. Whalen was coming abroad? She arrived last night on the Jersey boat, and saw Uncle and Miss Clara Emily on the ramparts through her marine glasses. She hunted us up at once, for she says that affair must stop right where it is. She asked if you approved of Lee, and when I told her that you did, she said then she had nothing to say. Lee introduced her to Mr. Peters, and she sent him straight to bed and had them poultice his chest and mustard-plaster his back, for she says his cold may run into anything. I took her up to Clara, and she sent out for sweet oil, and stopped the china straw, and set her to gargling. She says it's awful the amount she finds to do everywhere she goes, and she was in a train accident before she came to the steamer, and you ought to hear how she chopped people out. The shade in my room didn't work, and she put a chair on a wash-stand, and fixed it with a screw-driver that she carries in her pocket. Jim Freeman wants her to go under the automobile with him; but she says since she's a widow she never goes anywhere alone with one man. Uncle and Miss Clara Emily came in just then, and the effect was paralyzing. Uncle turned red, and poor Miss Clara Emily nearly sank to the floor. Mrs. Whalen advanced toward them as if she were a general leading a cavalry charge afoot, and said: "Well, so the old folks have been out sunning themselves!" Did you ever hear of anything more cruel? Miss Clara Emily looked blue with rage, and said she must go to Clara, and Mrs. Whalen said: "John, come with me," and took Uncle off behind some palms, and Lee and I went away so as not to be anywhere when he came out.

We didn't come back until nearly six, and Lee said he supposed we'd find Uncle and Mr. Peters learning to play "old maid"; but when we came in, Uncle was reading a New York paper about a month old, and Mrs. Whalen had gone out with Scott McCarthy to buy Clara a hot-water bag. Miss Clara Emily was upstairs packing, to take Clara to a specialist somewhere else. Mrs. Whalen came to my room after dinner, and said I must rub kerosene or vaseline into my hair every night for a month. I don't want to, but I'm so grateful about Uncle that I'll pour a lamp over myself if she wants me to. Uncle came to my room a while later and said: "Hum!" and shook his watch, and held it to his ear. I don't think he liked being broken up with Miss Clara Emily, but he only said that he was going out on the yacht to-morrow (that's to-day), and for me to consider myself in Mrs. Whalen's charge for the time being.

He went away early this morning with Mr. Peters and Jim Freeman and Lee, and Mrs. Whalen and I saw the Kingsleys off for Rennes at noon. I'm sure Miss Clara Emily felt dreadfully over Uncle, and Emily says she's more than ever ashamed of having such an aunt. Emily told me that if an Englishman came on this afternoon's boat from Jersey, to tell him they'd gone to Dol. She didn't want him in Rennes, because she knows two French officers in Rennes. It was not a very nice day for traveling, for there is such a wind they won't be able to have the windows down at all, and you know it's only fun when you have the windows down. Mrs. Whalen says she'd have the windows down anyway; she says she'd like to see the Frenchman that she wouldn't put a window down in his face, if she felt like it. I asked her where she was going next, and she said she had no idea, but she thought to Dol and Mont-Saint-Michel, as long as she is so near. She says it was a stroke of luck her happening here just in time to save Uncle; she's positive he was holding her hand through the marine glasses. She says it's good she came about Mr. Peters, too, not to speak of Clara.

"Mrs. Whalen has just come in to say she's going to Dol"

It keeps blowing more, and Scott McCarthy says that they'll be out all night. Lee will like that, and Uncle won't, and Uncle will see that Lee likes it and then he won't like Lee. Oh, dear! But I mustn't mind anything as long as Miss Clara Emily is gone.

Mrs. Whalen has just come in to say that she's going to Dol, so as to see the tide come in at Mont-Saint-Michel, and to measure out the ginger so I can make Mr. Peters the tea. I'm sure I'm glad she is going, for she makes me so tired and nervous, always hopping up to fix something with her screw-driver, and I want to wash the petroleum out of my hair before Lee comes back. He doesn't like the smell of petroleum at all. I offered to help her pack, but she doesn't pack. She wears a sort of night-gown for underwaist and petticoat together, and the front of her blouse has pockets inside for all her toilet things. She says she washes one garment every night, and buys a clean handkerchief each Saturday and Wednesday, and has a pocket for her letter of credit sewed to her corset. I think it is awful to be so very convenient.

Later.

She went and never said a thing about me, for it left me all alone with Scott McCarthy, and I know Lee won't like that at all. The mail came, and I thought I'd better say I had a headache and come up here to stay alone till Uncle comes back. I had all your letters and Edna's. Edna is so happy, and everything goes so smooth for her and Harry that I'm almost sorry some days that I'm Uncle's favorite. Lee wants to tell Uncle right out and be done with it; but I want to wait for a favorable time, and every time that things begin to look favorable something unexpected happens to make him say "Hum." It is so trying. Edna says she's getting a lot of things twice over so that I can have half, and she says she thinks we ought to be coming back so as to meet you. I can't make her understand how helpless I am, for I can't do anything with Uncle unless I'm alone with him enough to make him think that I want to do something else. And Lee thinks it is an outrage and says he has rights, too. I do think that if I didn't love Lee I would be really glad to have the world all women, men are so difficult to get along with.

But, you know, no matter what I say, I'm having a lovely time after all, and I *am* grateful to Uncle for having brought us.

Lovingly,

Yvonne.

P. S. It is ten o'clock, and the yacht never came in. If Uncle gets seasick in a storm, he'll never want to lay eyes on Lee again, and he'll *never* forgive me.

XIV

YVONNE TO HER MOTHER

Carnac.

Dear Mama: I'm just about in despair, and Lee doesn't know where I am. We reached Carnac last night, and Uncle is "humming" like a top, so to speak. But I must tell you all about it.

The yacht got too far out, and the new thumb-screw, or whatever it is on a yacht, stuck, and they blew and pitched until they pitched on to the Island of Jersey, where Lee and Uncle went ashore for Lee to send a machinist aboard. While Lee was busy, Uncle just quietly went aboard the Jersey boat and came back to St. Malo without saying please or thank you to a soul. He walked in on me and told me we were to leave for Dol the next day, and for Heaven's sake not to remind him of Aunt Jane by asking questions. I was dreadfully upset, but of course I never thought for a minute of reminding him of Aunt Jane, so I packed that evening and left a letter for Lee telling him please not to be vexed. We took an early train for Dol (it's always Dol in Brittany), and in Dol we changed for Rennes. Of course I thought that Uncle was chasing Miss Clara Emily when I saw the train marked Rennes, but I didn't dare say a word, for he never spoke but once between Dol and Rennes, and that time all he said was "Hum."

A Street in Auray

We reached Rennes, and I thought we would go to a hotel; but we changed cars again—this time for Redon. Uncle spoke again, and asked me if I had the Gaelic grammar handy. I said no, and he said "Hum." Then we reached Redon and changed cars again for Auray.

Going to Auray, Uncle asked me what became of Mrs. Whalen, and when I told him that she went to Mont-Saint-Michel, he said her husband was a lucky man to be dead. Then we came to Auray and changed cars for Plouharnel, and I began to wonder why we didn't run off the end of Brittany into the sea. We reached Plouharnel about four in the afternoon, and took a tram for Carnac at once, and when we reached Carnac Uncle said to pardon the personality of the statement, but that he never again would try to keep up with the eternal activity of a young person. I thought that that was pretty hard when I didn't even know where we were going, but I didn't say anything, and when he went to wash, I gave the waiter an extra tip to feed us quickly. After Uncle ate, we went out and walked around Carnac a very little and saw all the people in their black velvet hat-ribbons and short jackets; but when I said they looked picturesque, Uncle said that they looked like darned fools, so we came home, and now we are going to bed. I have written Lee, but I don't know when he will get it, because of course it will have to go backward through all these changes.

"When he went to wash I gave the waiter an extra tip to feed us quickly"

(NEXT DAY)

Carnac.

Dearest Mama: Uncle woke up ever so much better this morning, and told me that he pitied any poor wretch who has ever been sicker than he was on "that d———d yacht." He said, too, that any one who could suppose for a minute that he should have any serious intentions toward such a woman as Miss Clara Emily would be even more of an utter idiot than Mrs. Whalen appeared to be. He said, too, that the ticket-agent who told him that Carnac was an easy place to go to, ought to be strangled by the first traveler who got back alive from the effects of believing him to be telling the truth. He said, too, that if he survived Europe and reached home again, he'd get in a bathtub and know when he was well off for one while. He said, too, that when he had once looked around the Stone Age he was going to head for Paris with a speed which he rather guessed would cause the natives to open their eyes.

"Broke the bell-rope ordering breakfast"

Then he went to his room and broke the bell-rope ordering breakfast.

After breakfast we went to walk and saw more stone walls than I ever saw before. There isn't a wooden house or fence in the whole of Brittany, I believe. We walked to a tiny village called St. Columban's, and climbed the tower of the little church. There was a fine view, but Uncle said he could smell the oysters for miles around, so we came down right off and walked back. There was a girl who said she would drive us all over in the afternoon, and let us take the night train from Auray; so we returned to the hotel and had an early lunch, and then she came to the door with a shaky old thing like a carry-all and a fat little horse, and we started.

Mama, you never saw anything like Uncle. Everything was wrong at first—every living thing, and the one saving grace of the situation was that the girl who drove couldn't speak English. But after a while we came to the first menhirs, and Uncle just about went into a fit. They are the most curious things I ever saw, for they stand in parallel rows miles long and every one is resting on its little end and has been resting on its little end for thousands of years. At the first glance Uncle said they were arranged so just for tourists; but he got out and walked around them and tried to shake one or two, and then he said he wouldn't have missed seeing them for the world and that he should never regret coming to Europe as long as he might live hereafter. He was perfectly lovely for a while after that, and we looked at dolmens and cromlechs the whole afternoon, and sometimes we thought they were hay-mows when we saw them far ahead and sometimes we thought they were houses. We only had one unfortunate time, and that was when we had to ferry over the Crach. The ferry was on the other side, and that upset Uncle right away and he asked me if my experience had ever led me to a ferry that was *not* on the other side. They took nearly half an hour to bring it across, and Uncle said that it would be a great day for Europe if she ever learned what t-i-m-e spelt, and he looked at me as if I were Europe while he said it. They are building a bridge over the Crach, and as soon as we embarked on the rickety old ferry, it blew in between two of the piers and wedged tight, with us on it. Uncle asked me if I was going to have the face to tell him that we were not stuck and were not going to be stuck there indefinitely, and I really didn't know *what* to answer. The men in the boat hollered and hauled and swore in Gaelic, and finally we were free for fifty feet, and then the tide blew us in between two other piers. Uncle said he could but feel that being stuck twice on the same ferry was a poor reward for a kind-hearted man who was trying to the best of his ability to give some species of instructive amusement to an innocent girl, and then he looked severely at the setting sun while we came loose again and progressed fifty feet more. A great, thick wave came then and broke over the horse and smashed us in so hard and fast that I was honestly scared. Uncle was too mad for words. He said that he would just make one remark, and that was that if he ever gave me a chance to beguile him away from civilization again he would cheerfully and contentedly and silently end his days on any ferry which I would choose to designate to him. It was getting cold, and

I was so tired from yesterday that I just shut my eyes and did not speak at all, and when we came loose, Uncle spoke to me quite gently and was very nice all the rest of the way.

We were too late for the train and have come back to Carnac. I feel about done up.

(NEXT DAY)

Carnac.

Dearest Mama: Lee and Edna and Mrs. Clary are all here. Just listen. Lee looks like a ghost, and it seems that no one noticed Uncle go aboard that Jersey boat because Uncle went aboard by a gang-plank that's forbidden, and he thought that he was drowned, and they dragged the dock and sent down divers, and finally came over to St. Malo to break the news to me, having telegraphed Mrs. Clary and Edna to come at once. He reached St. Malo only to find us gone, and they have been tracing us with the automobile ever since. Lee is so glad Uncle is alive that he keeps grabbing his hand and shaking it and shaking it, and Uncle says I must not mention it to Lee, for it might go to his head, but that he is one of the few young men who have a heart in the right place, and that he has always had a special fondness for him ever since he was a baby. Lee thinks that under the circumstances we had better tell Uncle to-night, and we are going to. I feel rather nervous, but Lee says he can never stand anything like these three days again.

"He told Mrs. Clary that he had foreseen this finale to our trip all along," etc.

Midnight of the same day.

My own dearest Mama: Uncle says yes! He says he has been carefully scheming and planning to bring Lee and me together for years. He says there are traits in Lee which are so like his own that he cannot but admit that Lee is one of the very few men in this world calculated to make a woman happy. He told Mrs. Clary that he had foreseen this finale to our trip all along, and I do believe that he really believes himself.

The Brewers arrived about nine o'clock to-night, and they are so delighted. Mr. Brewer is so kind; he says Uncle must go to Locmariaquer and around that way with them. I reckon he thinks I need a rest. We told them about Clara and the locket, and I thought that they would die. Mr. Brewer says that never a day passes without their remembering something fresh which she must have overheard.

I am so happy over Uncle that I hardly know what to do. He says it has been the pleasantest trip of his life, this little tour with me, and that Lee must never cease to treat me with the tender care which he has given me all along. He says Lee must remember what a sensitive organization a woman has and never indulge in temper or impatience or strong language or sarcasm. Lee is very nice and says "Yes, sir," and nods every time. I do think Lee gets nicer and nicer all the time.

We start toward Paris to-morrow.

Your awfully happy,

Yvonne.

XV

UNCLE JOHN WELL CONTENT

"Well, Mrs. Brewer, this is certainly the only way to travel, after all. Comfortable, clean,—for if there is a smell, some other fellow gets it,—and no jolting. And now that I have that dear child established and off my mind, I feel that I can conscientiously give myself a few days of free and easy pleasure. I've done nothing up to now but consider Yvonne and her needs, mental and material, and although I love the child like my own, still I cannot but admit that a young girl is a great care. And of course you never can be positive that the right man will turn up. However, all's well that ends well, and I'm happy to say that I'm ending this little trip extremely well content. Some men might regret not having seen more, but never me. You see, Brewer, I am one of the easy-going, placid, serene type, and whatever turns up suits me perfectly. I guess if you ask my family far and wide you won't find one member to deny that statement, or if you do, you will just have the kindness to let me know who it is and I'll take steps to prevent their ever expressing such an opinion a second time.

"Fine view here. Good road. Believe I'll have a machine of my own when I get back to America. What's that island off at sea? Belle-Isle, eh? Dumas' Belle-Isle? Very interesting. We might make a little excursion out there, calling ourselves the Three Mousquetaires, eh? I'll be d'Artagnan; I always fancy d'Artdagnan. I tell you, Brewer, something martial gets up and stirs around in my bosom as a result of this trip—a sort of dare-devil, Robert-the-Devil, piratical, Crusader sort of a thrill. I shall never be sorry that I came. The trip has not been one of unmitigated joy. We have borne our crosses,—many crosses,—and yet I will remark—and I'll swear it, too, if you like,—that I'm glad I came.

"I've seen thoroughly every place I've been in. I've made my niece enjoy life, and I've made every one else with whom I came in contact enjoy life. I've won for her just the one man calculated to make her happy, and now I am headed for the one land calculated to make me happy.

"I'm glad that I came, I'm glad that I came."

THE END.